SL BEAUMONT

The Reluctant Witness

A Carlswick Mysteries Christmas novella

First published by Paperback Writer's Publishing 2024

Copyright © 2024 by SL Beaumont

All rights reserved. No part of this publication may be reproduced, stored or transmitted in any form or by any means, electronic, mechanical, photocopying, recording, scanning, or otherwise without written permission from the publisher. It is illegal to copy this book, post it to a website, or distribute it by any other means without permission.

This novel is entirely a work of fiction. The names, characters and incidents portrayed in it are the work of the author's imagination. Any resemblance to actual persons, living or dead, events or localities is entirely coincidental.

SL Beaumont has no responsibility for the persistence or accuracy of URLs for external or third-party Internet Websites referred to in this publication and does not guarantee that any content on such Websites is, or will remain, accurate or appropriate.

Designations used by companies to distinguish their products are often claimed as trademarks. All brand names and product names used in this book and on its cover are trade names, service marks, trademarks and registered trademarks of their respective owners. The publishers and the book are not associated with any product or vendor mentioned in this book. None of the companies referenced within the book have endorsed the book.

This novella is written using UK English.

First edition

ISBN: 979-8-230-12660-7

This book was professionally typeset on Reedsy.
Find out more at reedsy.com

In loving memory of Bella

Also by SL Beaumont

The Carlswick Mysteries

1. The Carlswick Affair
2. The Carlswick Treasure
3. The Carlswick Conspiracy
4. The Carlswick Deception
5. The Carlswick Mythology

Standalone

1. Shadow of Doubt
2. The War Photographers

Kat Munro Thrillers

1. Death Count
2. Cyber Count
3. Body Count

Prologue

Issie thought she might throw up. All morning, her stomach had rebelled, and now that the time had arrived, it was redoubling its efforts. Even scrolling through images on Instagram didn't distract her.

Her local bank branch's lobby could do with sprucing up, she thought, putting her phone away and gazing around the large room. The ceilings were high and could be generously called 'period features' if it weren't for the water stains in the corners and the peeling paint below the architraves. It was the colour too; a lifeless grey. These old stone buildings could take colour, and this one was crying out for a splash of something bright. Even a few large floral arrangements would be an improvement. She made a mental note to suggest it if the meeting went well.

The bank's atmosphere was subdued, matching her mood, and there were only a handful of customers lined up to see the sole teller partitioned behind the glass-fronted counter.

"Isabella Jenkins, the manager will see you now."

Issie looked up. The personal banker, wearing a neat navy blue suit, was standing in front of her. She gave Issie an encouraging smile. "It's okay, Mr. Hobbs doesn't bite."

Issie stood and ran her hands down her sides and tried to smile, although she was sure it came out as a grimace. She followed the woman through the open doorway on the lobby's right-hand side and into a small office.

"Good morning, Ms. Jenkins." The bank manager came around from behind his desk to shake Issie's hand and usher her into a chair. "Conrad Hobbs." The personal banker left the room, closing the office door behind her with a quiet snick.

"Hello," Issie managed.

The manager was middle-aged, with a wispy comb-over and small round glasses perched on his nose. He too appeared ill at ease, which gave Issie some courage as she lowered herself into the seat he'd indicated. The office was painted the same industrial grey as the rest of the bank. The Venetian blinds covering the only window were tilted downwards, and the single painting hanging on the wall was crooked. A limp fern in a large pot stood forlornly in one corner, and a coat stand opposite held a single brown trench coat. The whole room looked tired, a little like its occupant.

Hobbs returned to his seat behind the desk and picked up a file from a stack of brown manila folders. He removed the application form which Issie had spent several painstaking hours completing.

"A florist?" he said, peering over his glasses at her.

"Yes," she said. It came out husky. She cleared her throat and continued. "I currently work for one of the large firms who service the hotels, but I'd like to set up on my own."

"That sounds like a lot for one person," the manager said, reading her business plan.

"I won't be competing for the hotel work - I would like to make beautifully arranged fresh flowers affordable for more people," Issie said. She paused and thought through her rehearsed pitch. "I have well-established contacts with the suppliers at the flower market since I'm there most mornings, and I plan to set up an ordering and payment system online. I will sell directly to a number of stores, and I will initially make the deliveries myself, but you'll see at phase two of my business plan that I'm looking to contract a delivery driver."

Hobbs nodded.

Issie took a deep breath. "The loan is to build the website and to cover the fees associated with setting up the payment portal. My plan includes introducing a subscription service, where people can have pre-arranged weekly, fortnightly, or monthly deliveries."

"Premises? Will you have a shop front?"

PROLOGUE

"No, I can work from home. My mother recently moved to Spain, so I have the house to myself. I will turn the front room into my studio. I also plan to introduce and run floral art evening classes each week, more often at special times of the year such as Christmas and Mother's Day."

Hobbs looked at his watch. "Two thousand pounds, at 5.75% repayable over two years?" he said.

"Yes."

The manager sat back and smiled at her. "That sounds fine," he said, before signing the approval box on the application form.

Issie smiled for the first time that morning, already envisaging the floral thank you gift that would brighten up this office. "Thank you so much."

A muffled thud from out in the lobby made them both jump. Hobbs frowned and leapt up from his desk.

He hurried to the door and eased it open, peering out through the gap between the door and the frame.

The loud crack of a gunshot sounded. There was a moment of silence followed by a woman screaming and a man shouting. Hobbs pushed the door closed and leaned against it, the blood draining from his face.

"What's going on?" Issie asked, rising to her feet.

Hobbs looked over at her, his face deathly pale, and blinked as though remembering that she was there. "We're being robbed."

"What?"

"Get under my desk and hide," he instructed rushing over and pulling her chair out of the way.

Issie dropped to her knees and crawled under the large wooden table. She grabbed her bag and dragged the chair in front to help conceal her position. The door burst open and a man wearing a balaclava rushed into the room.

"You the manager?" he said.

Hobbs nodded.

"Come with me, unlock the vault and no one needs to get hurt." His voice was gravelly as though he needed to clear his throat.

Issie watched as the man pivoted and strode from the room, one hand hooked around Hobbs' arm, the other carrying a semi-automatic rifle that was pointed at the ceiling.

"I said, down on the floor now," a menacing voice in the lobby demanded.

Issie craned her neck to peek out through the open doorway into the bank. She could see five people dropping to the ground and stretching out on their fronts. An elderly woman was having difficulty getting to her knees when a second gunman approached and clasped her arm. His balaclava was pushed up and his face, contorted in a sneer, was uncovered. Issie gasped, clapping her hand over her mouth to stifle the sound, but the man helped the older woman up and led her to a chair against the wall. The woman sat and looked up at him, an anxious expression on her face. The man remained at her side, the Glock in his hand pointed at the ground. The woman fumbled in her large wheeled shopping bag, pulled out a tissue and dabbed at her eyes. Issie shifted so that she could see the teller's counter. The frightened woman was emptying her cash drawers into a sports bag provided by a third robber. She had tears streaming down her face.

"Hurry up," the man said in a rough voice, waving his gun in her direction.

Issie fumbled in her pocket for her mobile as the first gunman strode back into the foyer carrying two large bags. Her view was partly obscured by the manager, who stood wringing his hands outside the office door. The robber dropped one bag with a thud and walked over to the second gunman, who was still standing over the customers. He stopped in front of the scared elderly women for a moment before returning to collect the other bag.

"Let's go," he called.

Issie watched Hobbs start to creep back into his office, as though hoping that the thieves wouldn't remember that he was there. The gunman turned to him and held out his hand, his black jumper riding up and revealing a red and green snake tattoo winding around his forearm vanishing beneath the gloves covering his hand. "Car keys." Hobbs hesitated for an instant before digging his keys from his pocket and passing them over with shaking hands. The man hoisted the bags and the three bank robbers set off towards the rear of the building as the wail of approaching police sirens sounded from the street outside.

Hobbs slumped in the doorway, sweat sticking his shirt to his back. Issie pushed the chair aside and crawled out from beneath the desk. Hobbs spun around with a terrified expression on his face, but relaxed when he saw her.

"I'd forgotten you were there," he said. "Are you alright?"

Issie nodded. "You?"

He shook his head. "Not really," he said. Clasping his trembling hands, he took a shallow, shaky breath and stepped out into the bank foyer where the customers were climbing to their feet.

"Is everyone okay?" he asked.

Chapter 1

The bell above the door tinkled, announcing the arrival of more customers. The popular café was sandwiched between a dry cleaner and a hardware store at Fulham Broadway. Its reputation brought customers from all over London, and it was the favourite breakfast and lunch venue for many locals. Bella felt the rush of cold air that accompanied the newcomers, and glanced up, as was her habit, to check who was coming through the door. She let go of the breath she held each time someone new arrived.

Five young men strolled into the busy café, slid into one of the large red faux-leather booths opposite the counter and continued talking over one another.

Bella finished serving a customer at the counter, handing her a bright yellow cardboard flower with the number twelve in its centre. Laughter from the booth drew her attention. She studied the new arrivals for a moment. The shortest and most muscular of the group had tattoos running up both arms and disappearing under the sleeves of his short sleeve t-shirt. His bleached hair was shaved on the sides and styled into a shaggy mohawk. His cheeky, impish grin was directed across the table towards an attractive dark-skinned guy with short dreadlocks who had his head thrown back with laughter. Bella's gaze moved to the third member of the entourage who was shaking his head in disbelief, his long fringe swaying above a bemused expression. Seated beside him, a guy with a mass of blond curls was studying his phone, but her attention was captured by the fifth man whose long legs, clad in skinny black jeans, stretched out under the table. He was wearing a vintage paisley

CHAPTER 1

button-down shirt beneath a tan leather jacket, and his fair hair was cut in long layers. He looked like he stepped straight out of the 1970s.

She wondered who they were; five well-dressed guys not at work at nine o'clock on a Tuesday morning. It wasn't the first time they'd been in, but they were newish to the café. In the six months that Bella had been working there, she'd gotten to know most of the regulars. She recalled seeing the five guys in pairs or individually over the previous month or so, but never all together. Paisley shirt glanced across at the counter, as if aware of her scrutiny and caught her eye. Bella busied herself, taking the next customer's coffee order before passing it to the barista.

"Bella, can you go and take their order?" the other waitress asked, passing her with a stack of dirty plates and giving a nod towards the newcomer's table.

Armed with a notepad, Bella approached the booth. "What can I get you?" she asked.

"Depends what's on offer," the short tattooed one asked, flashing her a cheeky grin.

"Whatever's on the blackboard and nothing more," she replied in a cool tone.

"Down boy," the dreadlocked one laughed before adding. "Big Breakfast for me."

"Same here," the dark-haired guy with the long fringe said.

"Me too." Blond curls looked up from his phone.

"I'll have the French toast please," Paisley shirt's eyes dropped to the name tag on her apron. "Bella."

Bella glanced up from scribbling the orders on her note pad at the mention of her name. He held her gaze for a long moment. She felt the shimmer of warning run through her. Uh-oh.

"Hi," the tattooed one said standing and leaning across the table with his hand extended. "I'm Jack."

Bella gave him an uncertain smile but returned his firm handshake. "What would you like, Jack?"

"What do you recommend, Bella?" he asked.

Bella hesitated. She knew he was just being friendly, but she really didn't want to make friends, so this had to stop now.

"It's all good," she said with a disinterested sigh and then felt guilty when she saw Jack's face fall. He dropped back onto the bench seat.

"French toast for me too then."

"Coffee?"

"Yeah, five double-shot lattes please," he replied.

"Coming right up." Bella turned and walked back behind the counter, pausing to stick the coffee order to the chrome espresso machine and passed a second note to the kitchen.

"Boom, shot down again, Jacko," she heard Dreadlocks say with a chuckle.

Chapter 2

Liam woke to a quiet flat. He assumed that his bandmates were still sleeping off a late night at the studio. Scooping up a pile of clothes from his bedroom floor, he headed downstairs and loaded them into the washing machine beneath the messy kitchen bench. He ignored the dirty dishes stacked in the sink and stepped into the lounge to see if anyone else was up, but the two old sofas facing the large flat-screen TV were empty. A small decorated Christmas tree that Jack had arrived home with the day before, sat on the cluttered coffee table but added a touch of festive cheer to the room. Unfortunately, the room also smelled like five guys lived there, so he drew back the curtains and opened a window.

He pulled on his coat, slipped out of the flat, and wandered down the road to the café. He wondered if the pretty waitress they'd met yesterday, Bella, would be working. She was tiny, maybe five foot two, her dark hair highlighted with red strands styled into two pigtails. She wore heavy eye make-up with a dramatic cat-eye flick, was a little too skinny and clearly had something on her mind. He'd noticed her troubled eyes almost straight away, they looked haunted, almost frightened. And stranger still, she didn't seem to know who they were. They weren't really that famous, but most people in England between the ages of fifteen and thirty would recognise them now, especially when they were all together. Maybe she was into classical music, he thought, although her appearance suggested otherwise.

Bella glanced up as soon as he opened the door. Liam noticed an expression resembling relief cross her face as he entered the bustling café before she looked away and returned to serving the customer in front of her.

The café's décor was eclectic. Old fashioned leather booths lined one wall opposite a long counter set with rustic wooden boards laden with a wide variety of baked goods; pastries, scones, muffins and cupcakes. At one end of the U-shaped counter stood a gleaming chrome espresso machine, which hissed and whirred as a black-shirted barista worked his magic. Along the far end of the counter, facing back towards the door was a row of bar stools to seat those wanting counter service. The wall behind the counter had a large rectangular hatch opening into a bright stainless steel-lined kitchen. Two chefs worked at speed, cooking and plating orders before setting them down on the pass beneath hanging heated lights.

Beyond the counter at the rear of the café, ten square tables were set at regular intervals seating up to four people at each. The walls were covered in artworks, most displaying 'for sale' stickers. As usual, all the tables were filled, and a long line of customers purchasing food to go and takeout coffee snaked its way along the wooden counter and almost to the door. Radio 1 played over the speakers, and Liam caught an occasional burst of song from the chefs.

Bella and another waitress, whose name tag introduced her as Keira, worked their way through the line of customers, breaking away occasionally to deliver meals to those eating in. Keira had a friendly face and a big laugh, which rang out as she bantered with the barista between orders. Liam walked past the queue of takeout customers and perched on a barstool at the end of the counter.

"I'll be with you shortly," Bella said glancing up at him.

"No hurry," he said. Bella served her next customer before she spoke again. "Coffee while you wait?"

Liam looked up from his phone. "Ah, yeah sure."

She called to the barista. "Arty, a double shot latte for the counter here."

"*Si*," the barista replied.

Liam grinned and went back to his phone. Interesting, she feigns disinterest, but she remembers my coffee of choice, he thought. A few minutes later, a cup was placed in front of him.

"What else can I get you?"

CHAPTER 2

"I'll just have a croissant, please," he replied, smiling at her.

She didn't return his smile, instead turned and grabbed a plate. The corners of Liam's mouth quirked further upwards as he read the slogan emblazoned across the back of her black t-shirt; 'Dear Santa, define good…'

Bella selected a croissant using a pair of tongs and placed the plate in front of him.

"Thank you," he said.

Kiera was now dealing with the remaining take-out customers, so Bella walked out from behind the counter with a tray to gather plates and clear down the tables. Liam smiled as he heard her humming along to the song playing on the radio, one of *The Fury's* hits. As she returned with a full tray and pushed backwards through a swinging door into the kitchen, Arty paused from frothing milk and tossed his head towards Liam.

"What?" Bella mouthed, frowning.

Arty and Kiera exchanged a knowing look and laughed.

"You guys are weird," Bella said.

Liam finished his breakfast. She really had no idea who he was, he thought, which was refreshing. He'd always thought that he wanted to be famous, but now that he was on the way to being semi-famous, he found that outside of the band, it was getting harder to know who to trust; who actually wanted to be your friend or who just wanted something from you. To come across someone who didn't seem to want anything from him made a nice change. He was going to enjoy living around here, he decided.

* * *

Just after 4 p.m., Liam returned to the café. Traffic crawled in both directions and the pedestrians hurried along the footpath wrapped in jackets and scarves to protect them from the bracing cold breeze. The 'open' sign in the window was turned to 'closed' as the door opened and Bella stepped outside. She turned to lock the door behind her and jumped seeing Liam leaning against the windowsill. She put her hand to her chest as a fleeting look of terror crossed her face, but it was gone before he could fully register it.

"Hi," he said. "I was hoping to catch you."

"Yeah?" Bella looked suspicious.

Liam noted her expression with a sinking feeling, perhaps he'd misread things.

"I, ah, was wondering if you'd like to grab a drink later?" he said.

Bella studied him for a moment, indecision in her eyes before she looked down at her feet and shuffled.

"No sorry, I have a night class," she said, pulling gloves from the pocket of her overcoat.

"Oh, okay another night then," he said.

Bella shrugged and started to walk away.

"Can I walk you to the station at least?" Liam asked catching up with her in two long strides.

"Sure," she said, continuing walking.

"How long have you worked at the café?" Liam asked.

"Around six months," Bella said.

"And before that?"

Bella shrugged. "Here and there. What about you?

Liam smiled. "You really don't know, do you?"

"Know what?"

Liam shook his head. "Nothing. I'm Liam, by the way."

They walked in silence for a moment before Liam asked. "What are you studying?"

"French."

Bella paused outside a wholefoods store at the station entrance, its window decorated with an elaborate Christmas display. "I'll see you around," she said flashing him a brief smile before heading into the mall leading to the underground.

"Bonsoir, Bella," Liam called after her.

Chapter 3

Bella flipped the open sign to closed and pulled the café door shut behind her. Using a key, she secured the locks at the top and bottom of the blue door. The lights inside the cafe were switched off, and the espresso machine on the counter was covered with a large black cloth.

"Hey Bella," a voice called.

She looked up to see Liam, with a supermarket bag in each hand.

"Hi Liam," she said, extracting a hat from her bag and pulling it onto her head.

Liam put the shopping bags down at his feet and flexed his hands. "I don't know about you, but I always seem to buy more than I can carry."

Bella smiled. "You need a trolley, like the elderly."

Liam laughed. "I don't think I'm quite at that stage yet, thank you very much."

Bella's smile widened and lit up her face.

"You should smile more." He didn't mean to say the words aloud and inwardly cursed himself when her smile faltered and disappeared.

"Bella, how about that drink?" he asked.

"Sorry, I can't. I have to get to my night class," she said, motioning towards the station with her head.

Liam picked up his bags and fell into step beside her.

"What do you do for a job Liam?" she asked, her curiosity winning out over her desire not to encourage him.

"I'm in a band."

"Oh, would I have heard of it?"

"*The Fury.*" There was a note of pride in his voice.

Bella's expression remained blank. "I haven't listened to a lot of new music in the last couple of years, so I must have missed your band. Sorry."

Liam laughed. "No need to be sorry. It's kinda nice actually. But you do know some of our stuff; you were singing along in the café yesterday."

Bella looked up, surprised. "I was?" Liam nodded. Colour touched the top of Bella's cheekbones. "You must be well known if you're on the radio," she said. "You must think I'm stupid."

"Not at all, as I said, I like it that you don't know. But we must remedy that."

They paused outside the station entrance beside a large Christmas tree covered in silver balls and twinkling lights.

"Well, here we are again. I'll see ya." Bella turned and ducked into the station.

She glanced over her shoulder and saw Liam standing watching her go with a grin on his face. She sighed. He was probably a very nice guy, but she just didn't have room in her life for that right now. She pushed down a sudden pang of loneliness and decided to call her mother that night when she eventually got back to her flat.

Bella checked her surroundings out of habit, to ensure no one was following her, before holding her Oyster card against the ticket barrier and walking through the gate once it swished open. She skipped down the stairs to the platform and caught the next train to Earls Court, alighted, crossed to the opposite platform and caught the train back to Fulham. She hoped that would have given Liam time to get back to his flat. It would be awkward the next time he came into the café if he realised that she'd brushed him off.

Bella walked back out of Fulham Broadway station and hurried along towards the café. One of the best things about the job was that a small one-bedroom flat above the premises was available to rent at a discount. The only condition was that she needed to be available to open the café most mornings. As far as deals went it was a great one and it wasn't like she was doing anything else. The flat above the cafe was tiny, but it was clean and warm and had everything she needed right now. She was beginning to relax for the first time since arriving in London.

CHAPTER 3

Bella had just inserted her key into the lock when she heard her name being called.

"Bella?"

She froze for a moment before spinning around in the direction of the voice. Her breath caught in her throat. Fulham Road was congested; nothing was going to happen to her in daylight on a busy road, right? But she held her key ready to use as a weapon nonetheless. Her anxiety was replaced by guilt when she saw Liam weaving among the cars to cross the road from the pub opposite her flat. Behind him, she could see two of his bandmates standing outside the bar, watching them.

"Hey." Bella forced a smile, although she was sure that it must have come across as false because Liam slowed and looked hesitant.

"Did you change your mind?" he asked.

"Change my mind?"

"About that drink."

"Ah, no." Bella hung her head and scuffed her feet on the ground. "Liam, I lied to you."

Liam frowned.

"I'm sorry," she said. "I don't have a class tonight. This is where I live." She gestured above the café.

Liam's expression turned hard. "Why?" he began. "Actually, don't worry. I get it." He turned on his heel and began to walk away.

"Liam, I'm sorry," Bella called. "It's not what you think."

Liam kept walking. Bella watched him cross back over the road and speak to his mates before heading into the pub. Bella saw them glance in her direction before they followed him inside.

Tears smarted in her eyes as she unlocked the door. She pushed it closed behind her and raced up the stairs to her flat. She threw her coat on the sofa and sank down onto the edge of her bed, putting her head in her hands.

"Damn it," she muttered.

The timing was so unfortunate. She wasn't supposed to meet someone that she liked until she'd saved up enough money to get to Paris.

Bella reached for her bag, pulled out her phone and called her mother.

"Hola."

"Mum, it's Issie."

"Isabella, how are you, love?"

The sound of her mother's voice brought the tears back close to the surface. "I'm okay."

"You don't sound okay, what's wrong? They haven't found you have they?"

"No, nothing like that, I'm safe, at least I think I am." She shivered despite the cosy temperature in her flat and tried to infuse a lighter tone into her words. "I just wanted to hear your voice. How hot is it in Spain today?"

Bella tucked the phone under her ear and stood up slipping her cardigan off and hanging on a hook behind the bedroom door. She toed off her boots and pushed them in front of the clothes rack at the end of the bed.

"Mid-twenties and not a cloud in sight. Are you sure you don't want to leave that cold, miserable place and join me?"

Bella laughed. "So tempting, but I would just be a third wheel. How is Jorge?"

"He's great." Bella could hear the smile in her mother's voice.

"I'm so happy for you Mum."

"What about you? Have you met anyone in London?"

"You know I can't." Bella's voice took on a wistful tone. "Although, if I could, there is a guy, he's a singer in a band."

Bella let her phone drop back into her hand and walked through into the tiny kitchen, nestled under the eaves. She set her phone down on the bench and tapped the speaker icon. She grabbed a glass from the open shelf and filled it with water from the tap.

"Ooh, tell me more?" her mother said.

"There's nothing more to tell. He caught me in a lie about where I live, so I won't be seeing him again. But it's for the best."

Her mother sighed. "Issie, you can't keep pushing everyone away. You have to stop running sometime."

"They could still be looking for me, Mum. They burned down our flat remember."

"That was over a year ago and the bank robbers are now in prison. You

CHAPTER 3

have to stop putting your life on hold."

Bella looked out through the kitchen window at the pub opposite. Liam and his friends were seated inside at a table beside the large glass front window and had been joined by several other people. There was much laughter amongst the group, except for Liam who sat looking somewhat dejected. As if aware of her scrutiny, he glanced up at her window and Bella took a hasty step backwards.

"Maybe you're right, but first I need to work out how to feel safe again."

Chapter 4

Liam wasn't sure how he'd landed the job of keeping the refrigerator in the flat stocked. Maybe it was because he didn't want to eat junk food all the time, he mused as he walked into the supermarket in the Fulham Broadway station shopping centre on Friday afternoon. He grabbed a small trolley at the door and headed into the fruit and vegetable section. He stopped at a bin of satsumas and reached to grab several small orange fruit at the same time as a fellow shopper. He withdrew his hand with a mumbled apology and looked up to see Bella standing beside him.

"Hi there," she said, giving him a shy smile.

"Hi," Liam said, and turned away, walking towards the next aisle. He'd avoided the café over the last few days, and although he knew he would eventually see her, it didn't make bumping into her any less awkward. He wasn't used to girls saying no to him and didn't quite know what to make of it.

"Liam," she called, hurrying after him. He paused at the end of the row and glared at her from beneath the peak of his corduroy cap.

"Look, I owe you an explanation."

Liam shrugged. "It's fine."

"No it's not," she said. "My life is a little complicated right now, but I shouldn't have misled you. I am taking French at night school in South Ken, but only on Monday and Tuesday nights. It's just that I haven't been out with anyone in ages, and I guess I freaked out a bit."

"It's okay Bella," he said. "I was a little pushy."

"No you weren't," she smiled at him. "I was being standoffish."

CHAPTER 4

Liam studied her for a moment taking in her quirky attire. "I love your coat," he said.

Bella looked down at the burnt orange trapeze-style swing coat that she was wearing. "I got it at a great little vintage shop in Swiss Cottage." She looked him up and down. His military-style double-breasted jacket was unusual. "Do you like vintage fashion too? I noticed your leather jacket the other day."

Liam grinned and nodded. "Yeah, I do and I know exactly the shop you mean. They also have a branch in Shoreditch, which has heaps of stuff from the 60s and 70s. Have you been there?"

Bella nodded. "I used to work near there."

"We should go to the Portobello Road Market together. It would be great to go with someone who appreciates it, I've never been able to get any of the lads interested," he said.

"I'd love to," Bella said.

They looked at one another for a long moment without speaking before a man behind them cleared his throat.

Bella turned to look at him. "Sorry, we're blocking the way," she said letting the man past before starting after him to continue her shopping. Liam followed.

"Why are you studying French?"

"I want to live in Paris. I've always romanticised the idea of being a writer in my garret, minus the starving bit, so I figured I should at least be able to speak a little beyond my schoolgirl French before I move there."

Liam smiled. "Sounds like a smart plan."

Bella stopped and looked along the rows of breakfast cereals before reaching for a small box of muesli and adding it to her basket.

"What about you?"

"The band is my life, right now," Liam said.

"Do you make a living from it?"

"Starting to," Liam said.

"Wow, that's so cool. Are you guys from London?"

"No, we all grew up in Carlswick, down in Sussex," he said. "What about your family, are they in London?"

Bella shook her head. "Mum moved to Spain a couple of years ago with her new husband and my Dad died when I was young."

"I'm sorry," Liam said. "Do you go to Spain often?"

Bella hesitated before replying. "Not often. I'm not a great flyer."

"Just as well there's a train to France, then, isn't it?" he said as they reached the dairy aisle. He watched as Bella added a tub of yoghurt and a wedge of brie to her basket.

Well, that's all I need," she said hesitating in front of the self-service checkouts. "Liam, can we start again?"

He nodded. "I think we already have."

"So." Bella fidgeted with the handle of her basket. "Would you like to go for that drink?" she asked.

"Tonight? I can't tonight, but tomorrow night I've been talked into going ice skating with James and his girlfriend, who's in town for a few days. Do you wanna come?"

Bella took a breath before she answered. "Okay, although I'm a little rusty on the ice."

"That'll make two of us then."

* * *

December in London was magical, even Bella had to admit that. She'd been so busy rushing from A to B and looking over her shoulder that she hadn't noticed the Christmas season approach. But now, she saw the Christmas lights in every shop window and heard the usual medley of holiday music ringing out. Two young women sporting Santa hats, holding lidded white charity collection buckets, stood in front of the Christmas tree at the entrance to the station singing lively renditions of popular carols. Everyone seemed to be getting in on the act. Some of the black cabs driving along the road had decorated their interiors with lines of garish tinsel and even the trees lining the footpath leading to the station had strings of lights wrapped around their branches.

Keira and Arty exchanged knowing looks as Bella hummed and smiled the

CHAPTER 4

next morning.

"Anything you want to share?" Keira asked, leaning against the counter with one hand on her hip, during a rare lull in customers.

"Like what?" Bella asked.

"Like, what's his name?" Arty said.

Bella conjured a blank expression as the door opened and a burst of cool air followed the next customers in the door. "What are you two on about?"

"Denial, interesting," Arty teased.

"Since you're such a little ray of sunshine today, you can put up our tree." Keira nodded to a small box behind the counter. "It has to be the world's smallest Christmas tree, but at least the boss has stopped being a complete humbug."

After the morning rush, Bella lugged the box into the seating area and assembled the little tree, setting it up on a side table at the rear of the café, but where it could be seen by anyone who came in. There was a jumble of lights at the bottom of the box which she decided to string up across the front window, but first, she had to untangle the nest of wires. She was so engrossed in the task that she let her guard down for once and wasn't inspecting every new customer coming through the door, so she gave a little shriek when Liam appeared at her side.

"Hey," she said, her face breaking into a grin.

"Hey yourself." His smile softened his features and exposed a tiny dimple at the edge of his mouth.

"Coffee?"

Liam nodded.

"Have a seat and I'll join you."

She returned to the counter to write the order on a post-it note when behind her, she heard a whispered conversation. She spun around. Keira and Arty were watching her with bemused expressions.

"Arty, two double-shot lattes, please? I'm going on my break."

She stalked past her workmates with her head high and joined Liam at a table at the rear of the café, where they wouldn't be overheard.

"Are you still keen to go skating tonight?" Liam asked after they were seated.

21

"Yeah."

"Great, shall I pick you up? I mean, I know where you live, right?"

"Liam, I'm sorry," Bella began.

He reached across the table and grabbed her hand. "Hey, I'm teasing. We're good."

Bella let out a breath and nodded, noticing that he didn't let her hand go when Arty arrived at the table balancing two coffees on his tray.

"On the house," he said with a sly grin at Bella, setting the two drinks down. He tucked the tray under his arm and waited, his expression sobering. Bella glared at him.

"Hi, I'm Arty," he said extending his large hand to Liam.

Bella flopped back in her seat and shook her head.

Liam released Bella's hand. "Liam."

"Good to meet you," Arty said clasping Liam's hand firmly and looking him in the eye, something unspoken in his expression. "Take care of our girl."

"Of course."

Bella groaned as Arty sauntered back to the kitchen. "Sorry about that," she said.

"I would expect nothing less," Liam said. "It's good to have friends who care."

* * *

Bella found she was a little nervous when Liam rang her doorbell at six that night. She grabbed her hat and gloves and raced down the stairs, unlocking the door to find Liam waiting on her doorstep with James and a pretty dark-haired girl.

Liam reached for her hand and intertwined his fingers with hers after she'd locked the door, giving her hand a reassuring squeeze.

"Bella, you've met James, and this is Stephanie."

"Hi," Bella said smiling at them both.

"Hi Bella." Stephanie's smile was open and welcoming. "Is your flat up there? That's so cool. What a great place to live."

CHAPTER 4

"Yeah, I think I have the best commute in London," Bella replied. "I work there." She pointed to the café.

Stephanie laughed. "How lucky are you?"

"Where you are from, Stephanie?" Bella asked registering her antipodean accent.

"New Zealand," she said.

"So how did you meet James?"

Stephanie and James exchanged a grin. "Long story."

"We should go. Our slot is at seven o'clock," James said looking at his watch.

The Natural History Museum was floodlit, giving the impressive gothic structure an eerie glow. The branches of the trees inside the railings were strung with hundreds of tiny lights and one corner of the park at the front of the building had been taken over by a large artificial ice rink centred with an enormous Christmas tree decorated with gold baubles and topped with a large star. A temporary two-storey marquee had been erected adjacent to the museum and housed the skate rental centre on the ground floor and a lively café-bar on the top level overlooking the ice rink. More lights were strung across the outdoor second-floor balcony and around the perimeter of the rink. Music boomed from the speakers mounted on all four corners of the rink.

They collected their entry passes from the little wooden ticket booth at the edge of the path and made their way along to the lower floor of the marquee and joined the queue to hire skates.

"Have you skated before?" Bella asked Stephanie as they sat side-by-side on a bench pulling off their boots.

"Not really. There used to be a temporary rink erected in a square in central Auckland each year. I went with friends a couple of times, but I spent more time on my bum than actually skating. What about you?" Stephanie said.

"I skated a bit when I was younger, but I haven't in a long time. I'm hoping it's like riding a bike; you never forget." Bella giggled to cover her nerves. "Otherwise, I'm about to make a dick of myself."

"You'll be in good company then because I know I will," Stephanie replied, laughing.

They watched as the people in the session before them came off the ice and the door opened on their side of the marquee allowing them out onto the rink. Stephanie clung on to James as she stepped on to the ice. Bella followed and found to her surprise that her limbs seemed to recall the movements and she glided away from the edge as the music started up again. Liam caught up to her and linked his fingers through hers and together they followed the other skaters in an anti-clockwise direction around the Christmas tree.

They completed one circuit and skated to the side where James was coaxing Stephanie away from the edge, skating backwards in front of her, just out of reach. She had a look of concentration on her face and held her arms out in an attempt to maintain her balance.

"Look at you Steph," Liam said, coming to a stop beside her.

She glanced up at him and wobbled, wind-milling her arms in an effort to remain upright. Liam reached out and caught her elbow, steadying her. She gave him a grateful smile.

"So, it is just like riding a bike then Bella?" Stephanie asked.

"It would appear so," Bella replied. "Come on let's go together, we'll stay on either side of you."

Stephanie improved over the next half hour to the extent that she could skate unaided, landing on her backside only twice. They took a break in the centre of the rink and leaned on the railing surrounding the Christmas tree, which was when Bella noticed a group of teenage girls whispering and pointing at Liam and James. She glanced at Liam, who seemed oblivious until one young girl broke away and glided towards them.

"Are you Liam from *The Fury*?" she asked him.

"Nah, I must look like him, cos I get asked that a lot," he said.

The girl's face fell and she skated back to her friends shaking her head.

James smirked. "Thanks, mate."

"Does that happen often?" Bella whispered.

Liam shrugged. "Usually only if Jack and Dave are around to encourage it."

James rolled his eyes.

"Don't you just love this setting with the museum towering over us?" Stephanie said, leaning against the railing and looking up at the tower at

CHAPTER 4

one end of the floodlit building overlooking the ice rink. "No wonder they called it a cathedral to nature. Look, Bella, you can see gargoyles and animals carved into the stone."

"It's beautiful," she agreed.

"Come on, I like this song," Liam said, pulling Bella back out onto the ice and spinning her around.

"Bella," Stephanie called.

She looked over as Stephanie took a photo on her phone. "That's cute. I'll send it to you."

* * *

They got the last table at a small burger joint in South Kensington after their session was finished. The chatter of voices and bursts of laughter rose over the pop music playing from the wall-mounted speakers. Waiters rushed between the tables serving drinks, taking orders and delivering individual baskets of burgers and fries. Candles in glass jars flickered on every table giving a warm welcoming glow.

"I think I'm going to discover muscles that I never knew existed tomorrow," Stephanie said, wincing as she sat down.

"We should go again in a few days, while you still remember how to skate," James said.

"So Liam was telling me that you worked for the police Art and Antiques squad during the summer. That sounds fascinating," Bella said. "How did you get a job there?"

"It's a long story, but my father is friends with the guy who heads it up. When I discovered a missing Nazi-era painting at James's house last year, Dad brought him in to help recover it," Stephanie explained.

"Recover it?"

"My brother was trying to sell the painting but when Steph discovered its value, he stole it and disappeared," James said.

Bella looked taken aback.

"Then last Christmas, she uncovered not only some old jewellery but a cache of paintings that had been hidden in a French vineyard since World War II," James said.

A look passed between them and Stephanie took a bite of her burger, chewed and swallowed before continuing. "So anyway, DI Marks figured I must have some useful research skills and gave me a summer job doing research for some of their cold cases. In fact, I spent a few days at MOMA in New York looking into some more missing paintings, while the boys were there on tour."

"You were on tour in New York?" Bella asked turning to Liam.

He nodded. "Yeah, we went on a US tour with two other British bands and even had a TV appearance over there. It was a blast."

"I would love to go to New York one day," Bella said.

"New York, Paris, is there anywhere that isn't on your travel itinerary?" Liam teased.

Bella thought for a moment. "No," she said popping a French fry into her mouth.

"I couldn't agree more," Stephanie said. "So many places; so little time."

Bella said goodbye to Stephanie and James at the tube station and Liam walked with her along the road to her flat.

"I really enjoyed tonight," she said when they reached her door. "It's been way too long since I've been out like that. Thank you for taking me."

"I enjoyed it too," Liam said. "Can I kiss you goodnight?"

Bella smiled at him. "You can."

Liam cupped her face with his hands and leaned in to kiss her. When he pulled back, he tucked a stray strand of hair, which had escaped from beneath her hat, behind her ear.

"Would you like to go to the vintage market in the old Truman brewery with me tomorrow?" he asked.

Bella nodded. "Yeah, I'd like that. I'm working in the morning, though."

Liam kissed her again. "In that case, I'll pick you up at one," he said.

"Okay, goodnight," Bella said, turning to unlock her door.

Bella locked the door behind her and climbed the stairs. She kicked off her boots and hung her jacket behind the bedroom door. She wandered into the

CHAPTER 4

cramped bathroom to brush her teeth and almost didn't recognise the face looking back at her from the mirror. She looked happy and relaxed, for the first time in a very long while. She smiled. It had been too long since she'd gone out and had fun with other people without looking over her shoulder the whole time. And it was way too long since she'd been on a date. Her grin widened. Liam. Perhaps she did have a future to look forward to after all.

She opened the attachment on her phone with the photo of Liam spinning her around on the ice and forwarded it to her mother. Perhaps she would worry less if she saw that Bella was out having fun.

Chapter 5

Liam and Bella picked up a pizza and a bottle of wine and returned to her flat after an afternoon in and around Brick Lane exploring the vintage clothing market stalls. They sat together on the blue two-seater sofa in the lounge, with their food and drinks balanced on the small coffee table that doubled as a dining table. Liam looked around the tiny room and sighed with contentment.

"I had fun today," he said.

"Yeah, me too. Don't you find that shopping makes you hungry?" Bella said topping up their wine glasses.

"I know what you mean. Were you happy with your purchases?"

"Yeah, that dress just called to me," she said reaching for another slice of pizza. "What got you into vintage fashion Liam? Was it the music?"

Liam thought for a moment. "Not exactly. It grew out of necessity. My father left when I was a baby. My Mum was training to be a nurse, but she never got to finish, so she worked as a nurse's aide which didn't pay very much. Most of our clothes came from charity shops in Rye. You'd never know as she has a great eye and always looks well-dressed. Some of it must have rubbed off on me, as I prefer the old looks to the ones on the high street."

"That must have been hard, growing up without a father," Bella said.

"Not really, I never knew any different and my grandfather, when he was alive was great. He took me fishing, camping and all those sorts of things."

"So do you have anything to do with him, your father, I mean?"

Liam shook his head and gave a snort. "Nothing. Mum didn't hear a peep from him, no child support or anything until the band had its first Top 10 hit.

CHAPTER 5

Then all of a sudden, out of the blue, he got in touch."

"And have you met him?"

"Yeah, once and that was enough," Liam said shaking his head. "It was just before we went on the US tour. He'd read an article about *The Fury* in the paper. It was such a disappointment, he was a drunk basically, broke and thinking that the son he abandoned should support him for some reason."

"Unbelievable."

"Yeah, you'd be surprised how many friends you suddenly have when people think you're famous. Anyway enough about me," he said pulling her onto his lap and wrapping his arms around her. "Why do you look so anxious and then relieved anytime someone walks into the café?"

"What?" Bella said. "No, I don't."

"Yeah, you do. Who are you hoping not to see?"

Bella wriggled in his arms.

"Is it an old boyfriend?"

Bella shook her head. "It's nothing like that. I didn't realise that I came across so jumpy."

Liam shrugged and waited.

Bella sighed. "What is it about you that makes me want to spill my secrets."

Liam gave her a lazy grin, like a cat basking in the sun after a satisfying meal. "What can I say," he said. "I have a trustworthy face?"

She smiled and kissed him, but didn't look convinced. Liam pulled her close and ran his finger down her cheek, his eyes roaming over her face.

"You don't have to tell me if you don't want to, but you can trust me," he said.

"I know." Bella smiled, but she didn't elaborate, so Liam let it go.

"Now, tomorrow night we're doing a little gig at the studio to showcase some of our new songs. It's mainly industry people, but would you like to come?" he said.

"Are you sure? I won't know anyone."

"Of course I'm sure and Steph will be there."

"Okay, in that case, I'm looking forward to it already," Bella said.

***

There was a small crowd outside the studio housed in a white-washed three-storey building in North London when they pulled up in a black cab the following evening. Bella looked behind as a second taxi carrying the rest of the band pulled in behind them. One of the doors was flung open and Jack stepped out with a flourish. Several people rushed forward, thrusting paper and pens at him, whilst others stood back and captured the band's arrival on mobile phones.

"Wow," Bella murmured.

"Just stay close to me," Liam said.

Bella watched as Dave and Jack posed for selfies, while Andy slipped through the crowd, running up the steps, past a security guard, and through an open doorway.

"Here we go again," muttered James opening the taxi door and stepping out. He reached back in for Stephanie's hand as she climbed out behind him. Bella followed, with Liam bringing up the rear.

The flashbulbs of several long lens cameras went off as they passed through the wrought iron gates, crossed a small cobblestone courtyard in front of the building and started up the stairs to the studio. Bella put her hand to her face and ducked her head, keeping her eyes focused on Stephanie's back. They passed by the large uniformed security guard and were inside.

"Do you get that wherever you go as a group?" she asked wide-eyed.

"Only to official events. We seem to go unrecognised most of the time," Liam said.

"It's probably rent-a-crowd courtesy of Cam," Andy said, overhearing the conversation as they walked into a dimly lit room with a small bar area to one side. "That'll ensure some newspaper coverage tomorrow. Can't have the public forgetting who we are."

"I think there have been enough photos of you, Dave and Jack falling out of the clubs in the small hours to ensure that won't happen," James said laughing.

"Cam is our manager and forever trying to raise our profile," Liam explained to Bella.

CHAPTER 5

Bella looked around the room. A small stage area at one end was lit by a row of ceiling-mounted spotlights. A drum kit, keyboard, guitars and microphones were waiting for the musicians. There were a few chairs dotted around the edge of the room, but it was really standing room only. Groups of people stood drinks in hand, chatting. Bella felt young and out of place all of a sudden.

"We have to go," Liam said leaning over and whispering in her ear. "Here comes Steph."

Bella nodded. "Good luck or break a leg or whatever it is you're supposed to say."

Liam smiled. "I hope you enjoy it." He released her hand and followed the others towards the makeshift stage, pausing to greet a couple of people with handshakes along the way.

"There you go," Stephanie said arriving at Bella's side carrying two glasses of red wine. She handed one to Bella.

"Thanks. Have you been to many of these events?" Bella asked.

Stephanie shook her head. "No, I'm usually up at Oxford or working. I went to a couple of these industry things in New York and have to say, I didn't enjoy them very much. It's great that you're here, now I have someone to talk to."

"I'm impressed that you haven't got caught up in all this," Bella said waving her hand around, indicating the people in the room.

Stephanie grimaced. "I try not to. I mean, it's James's thing and I want to support him, but I have my life too."

"I know what you mean. Still, there are perks, right? Free bar and no public transport to get to gigs."

Stephanie laughed. "You make a good point."

"Good evening," Liam's voice boomed out across the room. "Thanks for coming to hear some of our new music. But first, we'll warm up with a couple of tunes from our last album. Enjoy."

"That's smart," Bella said to Stephanie before any further conversation could be exchanged because a wall of sound enveloped the room.

Bella watched mesmerised as *The Fury* played. She recognised the first two songs from the radio at the café and once again cursed her own ignorance of current pop culture. She noticed those around her nod their heads in time with the familiar tracks, but her attention was ultimately drawn to Liam. His voice rose above James's slick guitar riffs one moment, then was deep and gravelly the next. The following two songs were new, darker and edgier somehow, but still very much *The Fury's* style with Andy's tight bass track underpinning the music and James's soaring guitar. Liam closed his eyes and gripped the microphone, transforming himself as he delivered the lyrics with a snarl. Bella studied him, intrigued as he then launched into a ballad, his eyes searching her out in the crowd and a small smile forming on his lips. The final number was an upbeat song which left the small crowd clapping with enthusiasm.

"That was awesome," Bella exclaimed to Stephanie. "They are so good."

"They're pretty amazing," Stephanie agreed.

"What happens now?" Bella asked.

"Lots of shaking hands and kissing babies."

Bella frowned, not understanding.

"This is why I generally avoid coming to these things," Stephanie said. "They'll spend the next two hours or however long it takes, schmoozing. Let's get a top-up; we could be here for a while." She waved her empty glass at Bella before leading the way to the bar.

Chapter 6

Bella's phone buzzed pulling her from a deep sleep. She leaned out of bed and grabbed it from the floor. It was Liam. She answered with a sleepy hello.

"I'm downstairs with coffee and croissants."

Bella leapt out of bed, rushed across the tiny lounge and pressed the door release button for the main door. She poked her head out into the hall and saw him enter and start climbing the stairs. She left the door ajar and rushed into the bathroom to brush her teeth.

She pulled a jumper on over her pyjamas and returned to the lounge a minute later, to find Liam seated on the sofa with a newspaper open, sipping from a takeout coffee cup.

"Good morning sleepyhead," he said standing and gathering her in his arms for a lingering kiss.

"Mmm…" Bella said. "It is now. I'm so pleased that Kiera was able to open for me this morning, it would have been a struggle to get out of bed any earlier than this."

Liam released her with a smirk and passed her a coffee. "Help yourself to pastries." He indicated to a small cardboard box lying open on the coffee table.

"I'll get some plates."

When Bella returned from the kitchen, Liam was seated again, engrossed in the newspaper.

"Expect big things from *The Fury's* next album," he read, adding. "No pressure there, then."

He continued reading before he folded the newspaper and put it down. "Can I borrow your iPad?"

"Sure." Bella passed it across and watched Liam search several other media sites as she sipped her coffee, savouring the caffeine hit.

"All good?" she asked.

"Yeah, the general consensus is that we are upping our game, which is true. James and Andy are writing some great stuff."

"I know I said it last night, but you guys were amazing."

Liam glanced up from the screen and smiled at her. "I'm glad you thought so." Bella reached for a croissant as he exclaimed. "Look, you made the news too."

The smile slid from Bella's face as a cold dread gripped her.

"Show me."

Liam turned the iPad towards her. A colour photo of the group leaving the studio in the early hours of the morning filled the screen. In it, Bella was clearly visible smiling up at Liam whose arm was slung around her shoulders.

"No, no, no," she said. "How could I be so stupid?"

Liam's expression was puzzled. "What do you mean?" Bella leapt out of her seat and started pacing, wringing her hands. "Bella?"

"What have I done?"

"You've lost me," Liam said.

Bella glanced over at him and let out a sigh. "Liam, you must promise me that you won't tell anyone what I'm about to tell you."

Liam frowned. "That sounds serious."

Bella sat down again on the sofa and turned so that she was facing him. "It is. Deadly serious, now promise."

"Okay, I promise."

Bella was silent for a moment as she worked out where to begin.

"I was supposed to be a prosecution witness."

Liam's eyes widened and he ran a hand through his hair. "Supposed?" he repeated, his voice wary.

"The authorities couldn't protect me, so I made myself disappear."

"So your real name isn't Bella?" Liam's voice was cold.

CHAPTER 6

"It's Isabella, but I was known as Issie before."

"I think you need to go back to the beginning, what did you witness?"

"A bank robbery. My testimony was supposed to put the thieves in jail. The other witnesses claimed they didn't see much, but I was hidden and they didn't know I was there. I was the so-called secret witness, who was able to identify the men."

"Where and when was this?" Liam looked shocked.

"The trial was almost a year ago, the robbery ten months before that. The day before I was due to testify, my Mum's flat, where I was living in Chelmsford, was deliberately burned down."

Liam sat up straight. "What? Didn't you have some sort of witness protection?"

"Sort of. I was assigned witness care officers and put up in a hotel near the courthouse once the trial started. I'd gone back to the flat to pick up some extra clothes the night before I was to appear on the witness stand. I'd just stepped out into the back garden to check everything was okay when there was the sound of breaking glass and a kind of explosion. When I looked back inside, the front room was engulfed in flames. I snuck around the side of the house and saw what looked like one of the men from the bank standing in the shadows watching Mum's house burn."

"What did you do?"

"I scrambled over the back fence to the neighbours and then ran across into their neighbour's yard and got myself to the next street using the bins alleyway. I slipped around the corner to check on my so-called care officers and they were still sitting in their car. I watched as one of them took a phone call before they got out and ambled towards the house. They were in no hurry. It was as if they knew what was going to happen."

Liam swore under his breath.

"By that time the sirens of the fire brigade were sounding in the distance, so I ran several streets to my friend Martin's house. He drove me back to the hotel and I raced in and grabbed what I could before they came back. He dropped me at the train station and I hopped on the next train to London."

"Oh my God," Liam said.

"Seriously Liam, you can't tell anyone. If they find me, they might try to hurt me again, or worse."

Liam looked thoughtful. "How long were their jail sentences?"

Bella looked confused at the question. "The two that were caught got between two and three years. The cameras in the bank had been disconnected, so their conviction was based on being caught with the stolen money; receiving stolen goods. They denied carrying out the attack, they claimed they'd been simply paid to deliver some bags to a warehouse, no questions asked."

"And their sentences would have been much higher if you'd placed them at the scene."

"I know, but that wasn't worth my life. I was really scared and ran. I realised that I couldn't trust anyone except myself," Bella said. "And now you."

Liam gathered her into his arms and held her tight. Bella pulled back and looked up into his face. His expression was both sincere and protective. She reached up and kissed him.

"Liam, I really hope that I haven't brought trouble for you."

Liam dismissed her comment with a wave of his hand. "I have more questions," he said.

"Shoot."

"Okay, how much did they steal?"

"Half a million pounds, all of which was recovered."

"And they didn't take anything else?" he said.

"They came back from the vault carrying two sports bags, which I assume contained the cash. It was those bags, and one that the teller filled, that were recovered. I was hiding under the desk in the manager's office. They didn't even know that I was there, which was why my testimony was going to be a surprise. I think their defence team thought that I was just someone outside the branch who saw them arrive or leave."

"What were you doing in the manager's office?"

"I was sorting out a small business loan. The next thing we knew, we heard shouting and a gunshot."

"Did they hurt anyone?"

CHAPTER 6

"No, they shot a hole in the ceiling to get people's attention. The manager told me to get under the desk. I had just crawled under when one of them came in and marched him out to open the vault. They left the door open and I could see into the bank. There was one guy pointing a gun at the teller, who was filling a bag with cash, and one other who had the customers lined up face down on the floor." Bella shuddered. "There was lots of shouting and everyone looked so scared, especially a poor old lady with her shopping trolley, but they allowed her to sit on a chair."

"And then what happened?"

"The main guy came back from the vault carrying two bags and pushing the manager in front of him. I'll never forget the look on Mr. Hobbs' face Liam. He thought he was going to die. Anyway, the gunman took his car keys and they escaped in his car."

"What happened then?"

"No one moved for about a minute. Then the people on the ground slowly got up. That's when the police arrived."

"So how long have you been in London?" Liam asked.

"Almost a year. I worked at a café in Shoreditch for about six months until one day I thought I saw one of the people who were supposed to support me at the trial, so I quit at the end of my shift and moved out of my flat that night. I found the job at the café downstairs the next day, which has been perfect."

"So how long do you plan on hiding?"

Bella shrugged. "I dunno Liam. I keep hoping that they'll just forget about me."

"They probably already have."

"The thing is, what if they haven't? I've just given them a great lead as to my whereabouts. I wonder if that photo has been printed anywhere?"

"Bella, the chances of anyone seeing it are remote. You can't hide forever."

"I know," she said. "And you know the one thing that I miss so much?"

"What's that?"

"Flowers."

Liam looked puzzled.

"I'm a florist. The reason I was at the bank in the first place was to get a loan to set up in business on my own. I had big plans and I've had to put them all on hold."

"You should go ahead anyway, set up in London."

Bella stood up and began pacing again. "It's not that simple, that's exactly where they'll be looking for me, at the flower markets."

"Not necessarily."

Bella took a deep breath and shook her head. "Liam, I have this nagging feeling that I've brought danger to your door."

"You haven't," Liam said glancing at the screen of his phone as it chimed. "Look, I have to go to the studio this morning to lay down a couple of vocal tracks. Do you want to come?"

Bella shook her head.

"I'll come back here as soon as I'm done," he said standing. "Try not to worry, I'll help you sort this out."

Bella locked the door behind him and studied the photo again. Despite her attempts to change her appearance with hair dye, extensions and heavy make-up, the photographer had somehow captured the old Issie. It was there in her open and relaxed expression. She cursed under her breath and reached for her phone.

The call was answered after several rings.

"Hello," a female voice called, above background chatter and the clink of cutlery against china.

"Is Martin there?"

"Hang-on."

Martin came on the line a few seconds later.

"It's Issie," Bella said.

She could hear him walking, followed by the sound of a door closing.

"Issie, I'm glad you called. I saw your photo on-line."

Bella groaned. "Do you think they would have seen it?"

"I don't know, but first we need to talk about how you met Liam McArvey," he said.

Bella smiled. "Yeah, trust you to focus on the important stuff, not the fact that I've screwed up."

CHAPTER 6

Martin laughed and then lowered his voice. "Issie, you do need to be careful. I heard yesterday that Hobbs, the manager of that bank, was badly injured crossing the road. It seems the police are treating it as a hit and run."

Bella gasped. "No."

"You need to be on the lookout because Liam could lead them to you."

"Or I could lead them to Liam."

Chapter 7

It was a cold, grey December morning when Bella walked into Hyde Park. A long walk was just the thing to clear her head as she thought through her next move. Many of the trees were bare and the Serpentine looked cold and uninviting, but there were plenty of people about, rugged up in coats, hats and scarves. Runners jogged past her, along with numerous cyclists and dog walkers.

Two hours of walking along the paths and through the meadow gave her little relief. It was possible that no-one would see the photo, let alone recognise her, so perhaps she was worrying for nothing. Still a small voice at the back of her mind kept asking, but what if they did?

The other problem was that a music journalist or fan could try to find out who she was. She recalled Liam telling her how trolls on social media had a go at Stephanie when she started dating James. Someone digging into Bella's past and drawing attention to her would be dangerous.

The one thing that she realised, however, was how much lighter she felt after sharing her secret with Liam. It hadn't resolved the problem, but airing it seemed to have taken the fear down a notch. He was right though, she couldn't keep running, but she needed help to solve this and that meant trusting others with her secret.

She stepped off the train at Fulham and climbed the stairs to the ticket hall.

"Bella," a woman's voice called as she began walking through the station shopping mall. Her stomach plummeted, but when she turned, Stephanie was hurrying after her carrying several shopping bags. She had a stripy beanie pulled down over her ears and thick scarf looped around her neck.

CHAPTER 7

"Hi, Steph," Bella said, stopping and waiting for her to catch up. "Have you been Christmas shopping?"

Stephanie nodded. "Yeah, I'm trying to be organised this year. And James is so hard to buy for, especially when you're a student with limited funds."

Bella looked stricken. "I guess I need to think of something for Liam."

Stephanie smiled. "He should be easy, anything vintage, surely. Hey, do you fancy a coffee? Or is that like asking a baker if he wants a pie?"

Bella grinned. "I'd love a coffee," she said.

They slipped into a little café next to the ticket hall and placed their order with a Christmas jumper-clad waiter before taking a seat on a sofa in one corner next to a gaudily decorated tree. They both removed their extra winter layers and shrugged off their coats. Bella was thoughtful for a moment after they sat down. Given what she'd learned about Stephanie's background, she could well be the person to help her make sense of the situation she was in. Bella took a deep breath and prayed that she wasn't about to make a fundamental mistake.

"Stephanie, can I ask you something?"

"Sure."

"You were talking the other day about how you investigated and uncovered that stolen art," she began.

"Yeah?"

Bella sat back as their coffees were delivered by the barista.

"I have a problem that I think you might be able to help me with," she said. "Or at least give me some advice."

"I'll help if I can."

Bella spent the next ten minutes filling Stephanie in on the bank robbery and the events the day before she was due to testify.

Stephanie listened and looked thoughtful. "Does Liam know?"

Bella nodded. "I told him this morning after he showed me the photo of us taken outside the studio, which is circulating online. I panicked. If they somehow get to see it, I'm worried that they could use him to get to me."

"Do you know if you were held in contempt of court? Or if the criminals are still looking for you?"

Bella shook her head and bit her lip. "I haven't dared look. I never thought that I'd be in contempt of court."

"It sounds like a poorly planned robbery," Stephanie said.

"Perhaps," Bella said, "but they didn't seem like amateurs. Unfortunately, without my witness testimony, the two who were caught got light jail sentences for receiving stolen goods. I feel a bit guilty about that, but I was frightened at the time and ran. I couldn't trust the people assigned to help me and now I don't know how to undo what I've done."

"And they've never found the ringleader?"

"No, it's as though he vanished into thin air," Bella said. "When the police chased down the bank manager's car, there were only two men and the money. No weapons and no sign of the other guy."

Stephanie was quiet for a few moments turning it over in her head.

"I wonder if the bank manager was in on it," she said.

"He's been the manager at that branch for years. I used to go there with my mum when I was a kid and he was there then, so I don't see why he would all of a sudden turn bad," Bella said. "But, apparently he's in hospital following an accident last week. The police seem to think it was a hit and run."

"Really?" Stephanie said. "That's not a coincidence, surely."

* * *

Bella's phone rang as she climbed the stairs to her flat. She unlocked the door and switched the heater on before answering.

"Issie, it's Martin, I thought you'd want to know that a man and woman claiming to be your witness support officers called by the restaurant just now asking if anyone has heard from you."

"Oh no, what else did they say?" Bella sat down on the sofa and toed her boots off.

"Just that they just need to talk to you. And they had a copy of the photo of you and Liam."

Bella cursed.

"What are you going to do?" Martin asked.

CHAPTER 7

Bella looked around the flat. "I think it's time I moved on again."

Bella disconnected the call, hurried into her bedroom and dragged her suitcase out from under the bed. It took less than five minutes to pack her meagre belongings. The flat had come fully furnished, so she hadn't had to buy any furnishings or kitchen utensils. She was leaving with the one bag she'd arrived with. She retrieved a large envelope containing her passport, a new mobile phone and a small bundle of cash which she'd taped to the bottom of a kitchen drawer, and added these to her messenger bag.

Bella jumped when the intercom buzzed. She decided to ignore it and pretend she wasn't there. She crept to the kitchen window and tried to peer down into the street, but the angle was wrong and she couldn't see who was at her door. Seconds later her phone buzzed with a text. It was Liam.

I'm downstairs.

Bella cursed under her breath and threw her bag onto the bed before pushing the front door release button. She heard footsteps on the stairs and opened the door of her flat to find Stephanie and Liam on the threshold.

She looked from one to the other.

"We've come to help," Stephanie said crossing the room to perch on the edge of the sofa.

"Look, I know you mean well, but I shouldn't have involved you guys. I'm sorry," Bella said.

Liam glanced around the room and frowned. He took a step sideways and looked into the bedroom. He raised his eyebrows.

"Going somewhere? Were you even going to say goodbye?" He couldn't disguise the hurt in his voice.

Bella hung her head. "A friend from Chelmsford called me. My so-called witness support officers called at the restaurant where I used to work sometimes, looking for me, with the photo. I can't stay here."

"You can't keep running. Let us help you," he said.

"No Liam, I'm sorry," she said. "I've put you in enough danger as it is."

Liam grabbed her hand. "Stephanie has a plan, will you at least listen?"

Chapter 8

Bella sat in Andy's car as Stephanie drove to Broomfield Hospital in Chelmsford. The morning sun hung low in the sky. The small two-door blue Peugeot van didn't get a lot of use in London and was usually parked for days on whichever Fulham side street that Andy managed to find a free parking space.

"I phoned yesterday to find out which ward Hobbs is on," Stephanie said.

"Okay." Bella sounded nervous.

"There's no way anyone will recognise you," Stephanie said. "There's not a vintage thread on you."

Bella fidgeted with the short black wig and large round wire-rimmed glasses. She was dressed in jeans and one of Stephanie's warm jumpers. A modern rain jacket lay across her lap. "I don't feel like me."

Stephanie laughed as she paused at the ticket booth at the entrance to the sizable open-air car park. She extracted a ticket from the machine, drove through when the barrier lifted and found an empty parking space on the far side close to the exit. Bella retrieved the large bouquet of flowers she'd arranged using several supermarket bunches, from the backseat and carried it in front of her, shielding her face from the CCTV cameras mounted around the car park. The main hospital building had a new glass entranceway in front of the plain white rectangular structure. They entered a busy foyer with a large reception desk and a coffee shop. After consulting a wall-mounted directory they climbed the stairs to the third floor.

"You did well convincing Liam not to come," Bella said.

"And James; but I thought it would look suspicious if a group of strangers

CHAPTER 8

suddenly turned up to visit your bank manager," Stephanie said.

They located the correct ward and strolled along the corridor reading the names of the patients on the cards outside the rooms. Each room contained four narrow beds and had a large window facing onto the corridor. They continued walking until they came across a name tag for 'C Hobbs'. Bella peeked in the window. He was the only patient, lying in a bed on the far side of the room, partly obscured by a pale green curtain drawn around one side of the bed.

A peal of laughter sounded from the nurses' station further down the ward as the two young women slipped into his room. A look of fear crossed Hobbs' face as they entered. Stephanie pushed the door closed behind them and Bella approached the end of his bed. She was dismayed to see the bruising on his face and his left arm and leg encased in a cast.

"Mr Hobbs, I'm Issie Jenkins. I was in your office on the day of the robbery last year." She set the flowers down on the table that straddled the end of his bed.

Hobbs gasped as he recognised her. "You can't be here."

"Please, you have to help me," she said. "I've been on the run since they burned down my house during the trial. I have to stop them. I can't keep living like this."

"You don't know who you're dealing with," he whispered.

"Did they do this to you?"

"I don't know," he said.

"We can't let them get away with this. What do you know that you're not saying?"

Hobbs shook his head.

"Please," Bella said.

Hobbs studied her and let out a long sigh. He closed his eyes for a brief moment. "About a month before the robbery I was approached. I had no choice. They threatened my family if I didn't help them. All I had to do was cut the security camera and let them into the vault."

"But the robbery failed. The men were caught and cash recovered. Why did they wait a year to come after you?" Bella said.

THE RELUCTANT WITNESS

"The robbery wasn't a failure, it was a success."

"I don't understand."

"There was a valuable painting in the vault. They unrolled it to check they had the right one. It was Rembrandt's *The Storm on the Sea of Galilee*. It had been there for years. All that time and I didn't know what it was."

"But you said that nothing was…" Bella trailed off.

Loud voices sounded from outside in the corridor. Hobbs's eyes widened in alarm and he reached for the call button on the side rail of his bed.

"Bella," Stephanie said.

Bella rushed to where Stephanie had cracked the door open and was peering out of the room. A large man was at the nurse's station arguing with the duty nurse.

"You need to go," Hobbs said.

Bella returned to Hobbs's bedside. "Will you be okay?"

Hobbs reached for her hand. "Find the old lady and you'll find the painting."

"Bella, we need to leave, now," Stephanie said in an urgent whisper.

They slipped out of the room and hurried along the corridor, away from the nurses' station back towards the elevators.

"Hey, you two. Stop."

Stephanie glanced over her shoulder to see a tall, thick-set man rushing towards them.

Bella gasped. "I know him, he was one of my witness care officers. Quick, this way."

They pushed the door into the stairwell open and began running down the stairs.

"What old lady?" Stephanie asked.

"What?"

"Who was the old lady that Hobbs referred to?"

"I have no idea," Bella said, as the door to the stairwell crashed open above them and heavy footsteps thundered down the steps.

They rushed to the next landing and exited the stairwell through a door leading back into the hospital. The doors of the lift adjacent to the stairs were just closing.

CHAPTER 8

"Hold the lift," Stephanie called.

A male nurse in blue scrubs pushed a button and the doors sprung open.

Stephanie and Bella jumped in and Bella punched the close button. The doors seemed to take forever to move towards each other and just before they finally met, they got a glimpse of the red, angry face of their pursuer. Stephanie grinned and reached for Bella's hand giving it a squeeze. She was shaking. They watched as the lift rose two floors before the doors opened again.

"Is there another exit?" Stephanie asked, following the nurse into the corridor.

"There's another set of lifts on the far side of this building," he said pointing. "That way."

"Thank you."

They hurried, winding their way through the maze of generic pale green corridors, following the exit signs until they reached another set of lifts.

A minute later, they slipped out of the building through a different side door and after checking that they weren't being followed, strolled as calmly as they could back to the car.

Chapter 9

"I kept an eye on the rearview mirror all the way back to London, but it didn't seem that we were followed. Anytime that a car was behind us for too long, I changed lanes and slowed down, allowing it to pass," Stephanie explained to a concerned Liam once they were back at the band's flat. She sat on the sofa opposite Liam and Bella. A guitar rested against one wall and music posters decorated the walls.

"I should have come with you," Liam said, slipping his arm around Bella.

"We were fine," Bella said. "I've spent so long looking over my shoulder that it was actually good to do something proactive for once. Even seeing the man assigned to supposedly protect me didn't seem as frightening as I thought it would."

"You're beginning to sound like Steph, no thought for what could have gone wrong today," James said, sauntering into the room.

"James, can you grab my iPad off the charger?" Stephanie asked.

James passed it to her before sinking down on the sofa and pulling her legs up onto his lap.

"So the police didn't recover a painting when they caught the guys with the cash?" Liam asked.

Bella shook her head.

"Bella, I'm wondering if the old lady that Hobbs referred to might have been the elderly woman you saw in the bank the day of the robbery. Didn't you say that the robbers were kind to her?" Stephanie said.

Bella thought for a moment. "Oh my gosh, you could be right." She frowned. "You know, it wasn't so much that they were kind to her, they were respectful."

CHAPTER 9

Stephanie's eyebrows shot up.

"Did she testify?" Liam asked.

Bella shook her head. "Apparently she was too frail for that."

"Did they give her anything?" Stephanie said.

"I don't think so, although now that you mention it, the main guy walked over to where she was seated when they came back from the vault. I thought he was just talking to one of the other thieves," Bella said.

"Did she have a bag?" Stephanie asked.

Bella stared at Stephanie. "She had one of those wheeled shopping trolleys."

"You wouldn't fit a framed painting in one of those," Liam said.

"You would if it wasn't in a frame. Hobbs said the painting was rolled," Bella said. "I bet no one looked in her trolley. In fact, I think the police gave her a ride home."

"Right, let's look into the history of *The Storm on the Sea of Galilee*." Stephanie typed into the search bar on her iPad and began reading. "It's been missing since 1990 after a heist at Hannington Manor in the Cotswolds. It would be worth at least £10 million at auction today. A man called Tony Morely was suspected at the time, but the police were never able to pin it on him," she continued reading. "It says here that since he died in prison last year, his associates have been searching for it." She laughed. "Wow, look at those outfits, the 1980s really was a hideous decade for fashion." She spun the iPad around to show Liam and Bella the photo that concluded the article.

Bella leaned forward taking the iPad from Stephanie's hands. The group of three men and one woman looked as though they were posing for a music video. The men were all dressed in baggy suits, with their hair styled so that it flopped across their foreheads, but it was the woman who took Bella's attention. She looked familiar somehow. She passed the tablet back to Stephanie.

"You'd have fitted right in back then James, look at those hairstyles," Liam teased as Bella frowned.

"Does that article give their names?" she asked.

"Victor Anderson, Linda Carstens, Abe Murphy and Tony Morely."

Bella froze as she immediately recognised one of the names.

"I think I'll head back to mine, I'm exhausted after today," she said, jumping up. "Thanks for everything, Stephanie."

"It was no trouble."

"Steph's been looking for more drama ever since we got back from New York, so you've made her week," James said.

Stephanie scowled at him.

"You okay Bella?" she asked as Bella pulled on her coat.

"Yeah, I'm just tired. I'm on early start at the café tomorrow, so I'd better get some sleep."

"I'll walk you," Liam said, following her to the door.

"Bella," Stephanie called. "I really think I should mention this to my boss at the Art Crimes unit."

"You can't, I'm in contempt of court remember."

"I think DI Marks will see the bigger picture," Stephanie said. "He's got me out of a couple of scrapes in the past, where I'd edged a little close to the line."

"I don't know," Bella said. "You'll understand if I don't trust the police. Can I think about it?"

"Sure."

Bella kissed Liam goodnight at her door but didn't invite him in. "I really do have to sleep," she said.

Liam kissed her again, long and lingering. "Are you sure that I can't persuade you otherwise?" he said.

She smiled at him and shook her head. "I'll see you after work tomorrow."

She closed the door behind her and ran up the stairs to her flat. She locked the door and shot the deadbolts across the top and bottom. She leaned against it and sighed.

"Damn it," she muttered, walking into her bedroom, closing the suitcase and moving it out into the main room.

She spent the next hour cleaning the flat before flopping down on the sofa and making the call she'd been putting off.

"Hello, Issie." The warmth in her mother's voice brought tears to her eyes.

"Mum."

"How's that new boyfriend of yours?"

CHAPTER 9

"Oh, Mum. Something's happened."

"What? Are you okay?"

"For now. Are you sitting down?" She heard the scrape of a chair through the phone.

"Martin called yesterday to say that Hobbs, the bank manager, was in the hospital after a hit and run. Liam's friend Stephanie persuaded me that we should go and visit him."

Her mother gasped.

"Turns out he was in on the bank robbery, but only because they threatened his family. He said that the money was only a decoy, what they really stole was a valuable painting from the vault."

"You knew there was something odd about the whole thing," her mother said.

"That's not the half of it Mum. Hobbs said the key was the old woman."

"What old woman?"

"I think he meant the one at the bank that day. Stephanie did some research into the painting and it was stolen by an associate of Linda Carstens in 1990. The thing is Mum I wonder if she was the old lady at the bank that day."

There was silence from the other end of the phone.

"Mum, did you hear what I said? My grandmother is somehow involved."

"Oh my God, Issie. That woman is pure evil, even your father thought so."

"My only memory of her is when she screamed at you at Dad's funeral."

"Do you remember that?"

"Yeah, I was eight and she terrified me."

"That's why I changed your surname. I wanted to erase any link to your grandmother and her criminal lifestyle."

"She didn't look familiar, but then again I haven't seen her in years," Bella said. "Do you think she knows it was me who was at the bank and that I was going to testify? With the photo of me and Liam circulating it's only a matter of time before she finds me."

"I don't know." Her mother's voice was a whisper. "But if it was her she would have been worried that you might have recognised her."

"Martin said that a man and woman stopped by the restaurant asking questions and showing the photo yesterday," Bella said.

"Oh, Issie."

"I have to leave here," Bella said, coming to a decision." Liam's band is on the brink of something big and the last thing he needs is it getting out that his girlfriend has a murky past or worse."

"Come and stay with me. She'll never find you here. There's nothing in my old name."

"But I don't want to lead her to you. She's caused you enough pain. No, I need to stop running," Bella said.

"What are you going to do, Issie? Don't do anything stupid," her mother cautioned.

Chapter 10

Liam ran down the front steps of the studio the next morning and hitched up the collar of his coat. He crossed the cobblestones on the forecourt and walked through the main gates before striding to the small, but well-stocked 7Eleven at the end of the street. He purchased a carton of orange juice and downed half in one long swallow. His vocal cords were suffering from singing for several days straight as they worked on the new songs and he found that orange juice seemed to help. He strolled back towards the studio.

As he passed through the wrought iron gates, he dug his phone from his pocket and was looking at the screen when he felt someone grab him from behind and shove him hard up against the inside wall of the courtyard. The carton of orange juice fell from his grip and burst open on the ground, the sunshine yellow liquid running in tracks amongst the cobblestones.

"Where is she?"

"Who?" Liam asked, pocketing his phone and pushing the guy away.

The tall, muscular man, his head covered in a black knitted beanie, responded by backhanding him across the face. Liam's head snapped to the side from the impact of the blow.

"Issie Jenkins."

Liam straightened and wiped the back of his hand across his mouth. It came away with a streak of blood.

"Who?" Liam repeated, clenching his fists at his side.

The man landed a punch to his abdomen, followed by another blow to his face. Liam felt blood begin to stream from his nose.

"Hey, what are you doing?" Jack called from the top of the studio stairs.

"You tell her we'll find her," the man said giving Liam another shove, before sprinting out into the street and jumping into a car idling at the curb.

Liam slumped against the wall as Jack ran past him. Jack gave chase, thumping his fist on the rear door as the car pulled away. He returned to the courtyard a few seconds later and helped Liam back inside. They limped along a corridor lined with framed photographs of successful musicians who'd recorded there, to a door labelled 'Studio 4' at the far end of the hallway.

James and Andy set their guitars down and rushed over when Liam entered the room supported by Jack. Microphones and leads were scattered among the band's guitars, keyboards and drum kit in the small room. From behind a wall of glass at one end of the room, they heard a muffled curse and Dave hurried out to join them.

"What happened?" Andy asked.

"Some guy was beating Liam up. I chased him off," Jack said helping Liam on to a chair.

"I'll call the police," Dave said pulling his phone out of a pocket.

"Wait." James held his hand up. "Was it about Bella?"

Liam nodded as he accepted the towel that Jack handed to him and held it to his nose.

"Let me call Steph first. I think she was going to involve DI Marks," James said, pulling his phone out of his pocket.

"What's going on?" Andy asked.

"I think you need to fill us in, mate," Jack said.

"I will, once I get cleaned up," Liam said. "But first I need to warn Bella."

Liam stood retrieving his phone and tapped Bella's name. The phone rang before going to voicemail. He tried again.

Across the room, he could see James talking to Stephanie. Liam pointed at his phone and shook his head. James finished his call.

"Stephanie's going to go and see her now. They'll call Marks together."

* * *

CHAPTER 10

Bella dragged her suitcase downstairs and left it on the bottom tread, while she slipped an envelope containing the flat keys into the café's letterbox for the owner, along with a note apologising for leaving at such short notice. She pulled the door closed behind her as a white Renault pulled up at the curb. She checked the registration number against the app on her phone before opening the door to the back seat and lifting her bag in.

"Could you stop around the corner on your left up here for a second, so I can drop something off?" she asked.

"Sure," the driver said, merging with the traffic before turning left off Fulham Road.

Bella jumped out, leaving the car door open, and slipped an envelope through the letterbox flap in the door of Liam's flat.

* * *

Stephanie had just answered a call from Liam when she heard the mail slot rattle. She ran down the stairs and saw an envelope addressed to Liam lying on the mat inside the front door.

"Hang on Liam," she said.

She tucked her phone between her shoulder and ear and unlocked the front door. Bella was getting into the back seat of a car wearing a long coat and the short black wig she'd worn to the hospital.

"Bella, wait," Stephanie called. But it was too late. The car pulled away and turned the corner.

"Steph, are you still there?" Liam said. "James said you're going to Bella's flat to call DI Marks."

"Too late, she just posted you a note and left in an Uber," Stephanie said. "Are you okay? James said someone attacked you."

Liam was silent for a moment. "Yeah, I'm fine. Open the letter Steph, and read it to me."

"Are you sure?"

"Yeah."

Stephanie walked back inside and pushed the door shut with her foot. She padded into the lounge, dropped down onto the sofa and opened the envelope, withdrawing a single sheet of paper. She began to read. "Liam, I was shocked to realise that the woman in the photo that Stephanie found last night, the one called Linda Carstens, was, is, my grandmother. We've had nothing to do with her since my Dad died. I'm so sorry to have involved you and your friends in this, but she's dangerous. You guys are on the cusp of greatness and the last thing you need is me bringing trouble. I need to get out of your life and you need to let me go. Take care, Liam. I wish you all the best. Love Bella."

Liam swore.

"Where will she be going?" Stephanie asked. "To her mother in Spain?"

Liam thought for a long moment. "No, Paris. She's been learning French and she told me it was her dream to live in Paris. Meet me at Kings Cross – that's where she'll be headed, for the Eurostar."

"Not the airport?" Stephanie said.

"No, she's not a fan of flying."

Chapter 11

Stephanie met Liam and James at the side entrance to Eurostar Terminal. The electric doors swished open and they entered the station. The vaulted pale blue steel roof arched overhead and at the far end, red brickwork framed the main concourse. An enormous pink tree decorated with silver balls extended towards the roof in the centre of the forecourt. A man sat at a public piano playing carols, attracting a crowd of onlookers. Passengers heading to Europe for the Christmas break wheeled suitcases towards the international departures area.

"Ow, that looks sore," Stephanie said, peering at Liam. His right eye was puffed up and his cheekbone swollen and shiny.

"I've felt better," Liam agreed. "Any sign of her?"

Stephanie shook her head. "I've been watching everyone going through the security screening and she wasn't among them. I can only have been a couple of minutes behind her, so I don't think I would have missed her considering the length of these queues," Stephanie said.

James slipped his hand into hers.

"Let's take another look," he said.

They walked up and down the Eurostar departure area checking the faces of the people lining up and trying to see past the security gates into the waiting area, while Liam kept calling Bella's mobile.

He shook his head. "She's not answering and she'd not here. I wonder where she's gone?"

* * *

Bella was dropped next to the elegant red-brick St Pancras station, which looked more like a palace, with its towers and turrets, than a train station. After leaving her luggage at a Stasher's locker, she slipped through a side door and ran down the stairs leading into Kings Cross Underground. The digital sign above the platform showed the next train arriving in one minute. Bella hurried along the platform, glancing over her shoulder to make sure that she wasn't followed.

She caught the tube to Paddington and rushed from the Underground up into the train station. She raced over to the ticket machines and purchased a ticket on the next South Western train to Windsor.

She stood in the shadow of an accessories shop near the entrance to the platform until it was time for the train to depart. She hurried through the ticket barrier and entered the fourth carriage just as the doors began to beep indicating the train's imminent departure. The carriage was only half full, and Bella slipped into a seat near the front and keyed the address into her phone that her mother had given her, with some reluctance, the night before. The train shuddered as it pulled out of the station.

* * *

The sun was setting by the time the automated voice announced their arrival into Windsor. Bella stepped from the train and checked the time on her phone. She pulled her coat tightly around her; the temperature had dropped while she'd been travelling.

The grand old house was in a quiet lane at the edge of the village. The street lights were flickering and the houses either side were partially hidden behind tall hedges. The area had the comfortable air of privilege and wealth. Bella stood in the shadows opposite her grandmother's house and shivered. She recalled visiting once with her father when she was young. The red-bricked, three-level detached house looked foreboding then, and it appeared little had changed.

She studied the building. The front rooms were in darkness and there was a compact black car parked in front of the garage at one side of the house.

CHAPTER 11

A stationary camera was mounted above the front door, pointing at the driveway, so Bella decided to avoid approaching from that direction. Instead, she took a deep breath and crept into the front yard of the neighbouring property and stepped over the low wooden fence which separated the two houses.

She edged along a dark concrete walkway at the side of the house. Light spilled onto the path in front of her from a room at the back of the building and she could hear muffled voices coming from inside. Bella crouched down as she came to the lighted window and strained to listen. She eased up so that she could peek inside. The room was a lounge, with comfortable white armchairs and a sofa nestled around a glass-topped coffee table facing a warming fire burning in the large fireplace. A wall-mounted screen was switched on, playing a game show. Movement in the doorway caused Bella to duck down again as she glimpsed her grandmother entering the room, carrying a glass and talking to someone behind her.

Bella held her breath for a moment, hoping that she hadn't been seen. But the voices continued unbroken, so Bella peered inside again. This time her grandmother was seated side on to the window, talking to a man dressed in black trousers and a black jumper, who stood with his back to the window.

Bella's eyes scanned the room again before landing on a painting on the far wall. She gasped. It was the exact one that Stephanie had looked up the previous evening. The oil painting was striking; depicting Jesus's terrified disciples fighting to control their fishing boat in the middle of a storm, while Christ himself remained calm. It had to be a copy. Surely her grandmother wouldn't be so audacious as to hang a stolen painting in such a prominent position in her home.

"Issie, you might as well come in. You'll catch your death standing out there."

Bella's breath left her as she swung her gaze towards the voice. Her grandmother had turned her head and was staring at her through the window. Bella turned to run and collided with the man who'd been standing at her grandmother's side moments earlier.

"This way," he said, his voice low and husky, as he gripped her upper arm and pulled her through the front door.

Bella was propelled down a long gloomy hallway with soft runners underfoot. Light shone from an open doorway at the end of the passage. The man pushed Bella into the room.

Linda Carstens was still seated on the sofa. Her hair was auburn, styled in an expensive-looking bob cut to just below her chin. She wore a soft white jumper and wide-legged black trousers. It was her, the woman from the bank, except she looked more elegant and much younger. Her expression was hard as she studied her granddaughter.

"I could ask what you're doing sneaking around outside my house, but I believe that I already know the answer to that." Her gaze swung towards the far end of the room. "What I don't know is why it's taken you so long to come to me."

Bella was silent for a moment. "Why do you hate my mother so much? Why did you try to burn down her house?"

Linda flicked her hand in a dismissive gesture and reached for the packet of cigarettes lying on the coffee table. She extracted one and lit it. Bella watched as she exhaled a plume of smoke.

"You're not asking the right questions."

Bella frowned. "Why did you go to such an elaborate ruse to steal that painting, only to hang it in full view?" She flicked her head towards *The Storm on the Sea of Galilee*.

"That's more like it."

"Well?"

"Have a seat, Issie."

"I'm fine standing."

"Sit." Linda's tone brokered no argument.

Bella perched on the edge of the armchair closest to the door. The man stood behind her.

"That painting has been in my family for generations. It is rightfully mine," Linda began.

"That makes no sense." Bella was confused.

"What did your mother tell you about me?"

CHAPTER 11

"Not a lot."

"That figures," Linda said with a disapproving sniff. "I grew up at Harrington Manor. But my father disowned me when I fell pregnant with your father. It was 1976 and I was unmarried. Times were still a little different, especially to someone like my father."

"You expect me to feel sorry for you, is that it?"

"I expect you to be quiet and listen."

Bella bit down on her bottom lip to stop her next retort from slipping out.

"I fell in with a wild crowd after my father threw me out leaving me with a baby to support on my own. They were a bunch of similarly disaffected people who basically stole things to order. I went along with it until I fell out with Tony, my on-and-off boyfriend. Tony thought he'd make me pay by taking something precious from my father's home." Linda glanced at the painting.

"So how has it ended up here?" Bella asked.

"Tony died last year and had one little twist up his sleeve. On his death bed, he told me that the painting was in a safe deposit box at the bank in Chelmsford. I had a month to get it out before his estate and the authorities acquired it."

"Which was why the robbery was poorly planned," Bella said.

Linda looked affronted. "It wasn't poorly planned. It was perfectly planned. Those two were well paid to take the fall for receiving stolen goods and I left the bank that day with the painting tucked into my shopping trolley. As I guessed, no one thought to search the belongings of a frail, elderly victim."

"So it was you in the branch that day."

Linda nodded.

"What I didn't know until the case went to trial was that there was another witness and when I found out it was you, I was terrified that you might have recognised me."

"So you tried to have me killed?"

"No," Linda said. "Setting fire to your mother's house was only supposed to frighten you into not testifying. It worked, didn't it?"

"And you're sitting here with an extremely valuable stolen painting hanging on your wall, that's so arrogant," Bella said.

Linda smiled. "My dear, it's valuable, but it's not stolen."

Bella frowned.

"My father and I reconciled before his death and I inherited my share of his estate, including this painting, if it was ever recovered."

Bella sat back digesting this.

"So, why didn't you just wait for the police to uncover the location of the painting after Tony's death? It would have reverted to you eventually."

"What's the fun in that? And besides, I'm not getting any younger and that process could have taken years."

"What about the other bank robber, the one who was never caught?" Bella asked.

Linda waved her hand. "You've just met him. Say hello to Scott."

Bella swung her head to look at the man who had dragged her inside, now standing behind her chair, his hands clasped in front of him. The head of a green and red snake was tattooed on the back of his hand, its body disappearing beneath the cuff of his sweater. Bella gasped before looking back at her grandmother.

"And Hobbs, why did you try to have him killed? It sounds like he played his part."

Linda frowned. "What do you mean? Try to have him killed?"

"Hobbs was the victim of a hit and run last week."

"I didn't know that," Linda said. "Nothing to do with me."

"You expect me to believe that?"

"Why would I lie?"

"So what happens now?" Bella asked.

Linda thought for a moment and shrugged. "You're free to go. I just wanted to make sure that you understood, despite what your mother may have told you, that I'm not a bad person. I was simply recovering something that was mine."

"So I'm free to resume my life?"

"You are."

"But I have a contempt of court charge hanging over me, thanks to you,"

CHAPTER 11

Bella said.

"I think you'll find if you explain that you were frightened after you mistook a gas line explosion at your flat as a deliberately set fire, then you will obtain some sympathy from the court," Linda said.

"But you just admitted…" Bella began.

"Yes?"

Bella shook her head as loud voices sounded in the hallway. Linda frowned.

"Check that out, will you," she instructed Scott.

Seconds later four police officers, led by a large, balding, plain-clothes detective entered the room.

"Linda Carstens, I'm arresting you for conspiracy to commit robbery and receiving stolen goods," he said, before reciting her rights.

Bella leapt to her feet and moved away from Linda towards the police officer.

Linda stood and gave Bella a look of thunder. "You," she began as one of the uniformed officers led her to the door.

"You must be Bella. I'm Detective Inspector Marks," the detective said holding out his hand to Bella. "We spoke on the phone earlier."

Chapter 12

"Let me get this straight. You called DI Marks," Liam said. "How did you get his number?"

"I simply telephoned Scotland Yard and asked to be put through to him," Bella said.

They were seated on a sofa in one corner of The Café, owned by *The Fury's* bass player Andy, in the village of Carlswick. Outside, a light sprinkling of snow was falling and the sun was beginning to set. Strings of fairy lights crisscrossed the ceiling, candles burned in a variety of glass jars on each table and a real Christmas tree standing at one end of the counter scented the room with a fresh pine fragrance.

"Stephanie said that I could trust him, so I agreed to see what sort of confession I could get out of my grandmother. I met one of his team at the station in Windsor and they gave me a wire to wear."

"You could have been hurt or worse," Liam said.

"Perhaps, but I am so tired of jumping at my own shadow. These last couple of weeks with you have shown me what I've been missing out on by putting my life on hold because I was frightened," Bella said.

"You did really well," Stephanie agreed. "Marks is delighted with the recovery of several other pieces of art from your grandmother's home. It's closed a couple of cold cases for him." She looked around the café. "Back in a minute." She jumped up to clear the dirty cups and plates from several tables and rounded the counter to add them to the dishwasher. They watched as she returned with a spray bottle and cloth and wiped down the tables and straightened the chairs.

CHAPTER 12

Bella looked puzzled.

"She worked here last summer, so I guess old habits die hard."

"I really like her," Bella said.

"Yeah, she's great for James," Liam said, leaning over and kissing her as Andy set two steaming mugs of hot chocolate on the coffee table in front of them.

"Here ya go, enjoy. The others should be here shortly."

"Thank you, Andy."

"You're most welcome Bella," he said.

"Are you sure that your Mum is okay with me being here for Christmas?" Bella asked, turning to Liam.

"You're kidding, right? She's so excited. I've never brought a girlfriend home to stay before, so she's going all out. I have a surprise for her too."

"Yeah?"

Liam dug into the bag on the seat beside him and pulled a large envelope. He handed it to Bella who withdrew several sheets of paper. She scanned them and smiled.

"Should we start calling you Santa?"

"I owe her everything. It's the least I can do."

"What's the least you can do, mate?" James asked flopping down on the sofa opposite them. Stephanie dropped down beside him.

Liam looked a little embarrassed. "I've bought the cottage that we've rented all my life and put it in Mum's name. She doesn't know yet."

James leaned forward and hi-fived him. "That's awesome, dude."

"She's going to have a great Christmas," Stephanie said.

Liam threw his arm around Bella. "We all are. This is going to be the best Christmas ever."

The End

Acknowledgements

Thanks to Gary Smailes, editor extraordinaire for working with me on *The Reluctant Witness* and to Sarah Smith for proofreading. Jessica at Jessica Bell Designs created the awesome cover.

Huge thanks once again to my amazing launch team for their early reads and for helping spread the word! You know who you are but special thanks to Tresna, Gill, Eveie, Shannon, Graham, Melanie, Judy, Roger, Karen, Eileen, Suzanne, Kathy, Judith, Jackie, Karin, Susan, Helen and Milena.

This novella was fun to write. I've had the concept for a Carlswick Christmas story for a while now and I liked the idea of including some of the other members of *The Fury* in the action, so I hope that you enjoyed that too.

Thanks to Craig, Jude, Zak, and Scott (yes, you've had a character named after you at last!) for your support and encouragement of my writing.

Finally, thanks to all my readers, especially my Reader's Group whose emails keep me going when I'm head down, tapping away on the keyboard.

A Note from the Author

Thank you for reading *The Reluctant Witness*! If you enjoyed it, I'd appreciate a short review on the site where you purchased the book. Reviews are the best way for indie authors to increase the discoverability of their books.

The Reluctant Witness is part of *The Carlswick Mysteries*, a series of mystery novels that delve into art crimes, such as Nazi looting, antiquities trafficking, and rare manuscript theft. The series is set in Europe with a Kiwi protagonist and her English rock guitarist boyfriend thrown into the midst of the intrigue.

You can join my Reader's Group to be the first to hear of new releases, competitions and discounts by visiting my website at https://www.slbeaumont.com

Keep reading for the first chapters of Book #1, *The Carlswick Affair* and the award-winning standalone novel, *Shadow of Doubt*.

Enjoy!

The Carlswick Affair

Prologue

Nationalgalerie, Berlin, March 1939

The clock in the old tower chimed eight times and fell silent. The neoclassical building was in darkness, except for a pool of light emanating from a single lamp burning in the curator's office.

A loud pounding on the front doors echoed through the stillness of the night. Karl Hoffman was startled and jumped up from his desk. Who could it be at this hour?

The pounding sounded again, louder and this time accompanied by shouting: "By order of the Führer, open up!"

"I'm coming," muttered Hoffman as he hurried down a sweeping staircase to the foyer. The moon shone in through the large picture windows, bathing the foyer in an eerie light. The normally benign marble statues standing in a semi-circle facing the doors, now cast menacing shadows. Hoffman, a short, slightly overweight, balding man in his mid-forties, shuddered and felt his heart racing as he began the process of unlocking the bolts and lifting the heavy metal bar from across the massive wooden doors. Inserting a large metal key in the lock, he had barely finished turning it when the doors were pushed open with such force that he was sent sprawling backwards across the marble floor.

Heavily armed soldiers filed into the foyer and stood to attention as an officer strode in and stood over him.

"Hoffman?" he sneered. He cut an imposing figure in his Nazi uniform. He was over six foot tall, with cropped blond hair protruding from under his peaked cap.

"Yes," Hoffman replied, the icy hand of fear clutching at his throat. Having your name known by a Nazi officer was never a good thing.

The officer thrust a piece of paper towards him. "I have orders to gather all the remaining Degenerate Art that is in your possession."

Hoffman scrambled to his feet, sweat beading on his forehead. "Now? At this hour?" he asked.

"Are you questioning an order from our Führer?" the officer shouted as he began to peel off his black leather gloves.

Hoffman held up his hands and took a step backwards eyeing the soldiers' rifles uneasily. He, like many Germans, had heard the rumours of people who disagreed with a request from Hitler, disappearing, never to be seen again. "No. No – of course not. I am just surprised not to have been given more notice. I have no staff here at this hour to assist."

"This is why I have brought my men." The officer smiled a cold, cruel smile. "Now, where are they?" he demanded.

Hoffman ran a hand through his thinning grey hair and took a deep breath to steady his nerves. "Follow me." *What would they want with the art and why suddenly at this time of night?* he wondered.

He led the soldiers down a winding staircase into the depths of the gallery to a large basement room. He paused, unlocking the door.

"Now, which pieces do you require?" He glanced at the document he had been given by the officer. It didn't specify, it just stated all Degenerate Art still being held at the Nationalgalerie.

"All," the officer said sharply.

Hoffman stood up straight at the officer's tone. He wanted to know where the soldiers were taking the artworks, but he was too afraid to ask. A few years earlier, Hitler had labelled all types of modern artistic expression as Degenerate Art, and called any artist who did not have Aryan blood a degenerate. Hitler's decree of June 1937 had given Goebbels authority to ransack all of the German museums. Along with works by German artists, his team had also scooped up pieces by painters such as Picasso and van Gogh.

"The items in this room are all by lesser known artists and have little value on the international market," Hoffman said indicating the hundreds of paintings stacked on their ends in rows along the walls. Shelving at the back of the room contained many books and row upon row of bronze and terracotta statues and sculptures, stacked there only because they had been created by Jewish artists.

A wave of nausea passed over him. He recalled the Degenerate Art Exhibition he had seen in Munich in late 1937 where 650 paintings, sculptures, books and prints had been gathered from German museums and were displayed in a way that made a mockery of them. Hitler had called the artists 'incompetents, cheats and madmen' and over two million visitors had flocked to see the exhibition that Hitler said showed qualities of 'racial impurity, mental disease and weakness of character.'

Hoffman prayed that this wasn't about to happen again. He, like many in the art world, had been horrified to see works by artists such as Chagall, Klee and Mondrian treated in such a dismissive manner. But they had been powerless to stop the exhibition, which had been the brainchild of Hitler himself.

The officer signalled to his men, who pushed past Hoffman into the room and began gathering the paintings and marching back up the stairs to the foyer.

"Careful," Hoffman couldn't help but call after them, his curator's hackles raised at seeing artistic treasures so roughly treated.

The officer gave a nasty laugh. "Oh, you needn't worry about that."

The first of the soldiers returned to the room, carrying out more paintings and sculptures. In no time the room was empty.

The officer turned to Hoffman. "Are there any more?"

"Only those being prepared for auction," Hoffman lied.

The officer studied him. "Very well," he said, and turned on his heel and marched back up the stairs. Hoffman let out a shaky breath and looked sadly into the empty room before closing the door and following the officer.

"Excuse me?" he called. He couldn't help himself. He had to know. "What are you going to do with them? Is there to be another Degenerate Art exhibition?"

The officer paused at the top of the winding staircase and looked down at

Hoffman with scorn and laughed. "Come, my friend, you will see."

It was then that Hoffman smelled smoke. He ran up the stairs past the officer, whose laughter echoed through the silent gallery. He pushed open the massive doors leading onto the front steps. There on the gently sloping grass frontage, the Berlin Fire Brigade had started a large bonfire and soldiers and firemen were tossing the paintings and books from the gallery's basement room onto it. Hoffman gave a cry and sank to his knees, watching in disbelief and horror as hundreds of works of art were systematically destroyed.

Shadow of Doubt

Part I

Chapter 1

July 10

"For God's sake, get one of the others to do it," I said, exasperated, as I looked up from my computer at my boss who was leaning on the wall of my cubicle.

"No. It's your turn," Andrew replied turning away, signaling an end to the conversation.

I sighed and stood up, stretching my back. Three hours straight sitting at a desk wasn't good. I had been hoping to squeeze in a trip to the gym after work to loosen everything up, but it looked like my evening was going in entirely another direction.

Hesitating only for a moment, I followed Andrew down the row to his cubicle, not willing to give in quite so easily. Andrew was a heavyset man in his mid-thirties. His thinning hair was cropped close to his head, but did nothing to detract from his good looks. He oozed charm and ruled his team of accountants and analysts in the derivatives division of the investment bank, Dobson Stone, with a mixture of fear and admiration. To be on Andrew's good side was like being bathed in the warmth of sunshine, but do wrong by him and it felt like being exposed to the iciest of winters. Fortunately, I had only ever felt the heat of summer, which gave me the opportunity to push the boundaries. And now was when I needed one of those opportunities.

"Come on, Andrew. You know that you're going to employ him anyway." I flashed my most winning smile at him. "Let's just skip this bit."

'This bit' was the tradition in the team of finally vetting any new recruit by taking them out to a local watering hole and doing a 'social' interview. The derivatives team was a close knit, play hard, work hard group and Andrew was a big fan of team players. Ever since the disastrous recruitment of an accountant named Peter, who had been hired without the social interview, Andrew had deemed it mandatory. Peter had passed all of the other interview stages with flying colors, but once he joined the team his lack of humor, aversion to socializing with his colleagues and propensity to back stab had caused major problems.

"Need to make sure he's not another Peter, Jess. And besides, William seems like the kind of guy who will appreciate a pretty face." Andrew grinned, knowing full well that the latter comment would annoy me and distract me from my argument.

Putting my hands on my hips, I scowled at him and practically hissed, "I can't believe you just said that. I will report you to the Diversity Committee. Maybe select me for my knowledge of the business or my social charm, but because of my looks? Give me a break."

Andrew threw back his head and roared with laughter. He had one of those loud laughs which made people stop what they were doing and look in his direction, in case they were missing something really good. Jimmy looked up from the next cubicle, catching the end of my rant. He and fellow Antipodean Dave were always quick with a quip and up for anything. They were usually behind the many practical jokes that went on at the office and they never, ever, missed an opportunity to wind someone up.

"Watch out, Scotty is about to blow," Jimmy called out to anyone in the team who was listening. Jimmy had an open, friendly face. At the tender age of twenty-four, he already had smile lines surrounding his mischievous eyes. He had the physique of the champion fighters in his family, but not the temperament. Andrew and I both glared at him. Still grinning, he held his hands up as if to protect himself and sat down again.

"Machiavelli's Wine Bar, seven pm," Andrew instructed and turned to pick up his ringing phone. I was dismissed with a wave of his hand.

I returned to my cubicle muttering about the appropriateness of the venue, and picked up my mobile to call my husband Colin. He answered on the second ring.

"Make it quick, Jess. I'm having a crazy day."

"I have to work late, a recruitment interview in a pub of all things," I said.

"Which one?"

"Machiavelli's."

"Okay. Good. Gotta go." He was gone. I wasn't even sure that he had heard me.

Jimmy and Dave stopped by my desk as I was shutting down my computer at the end of the day. Dave was the opposite of Jimmy physically, short and slight with a mop of messy blond hair, but he shared his friend's sense of fun.

"Where are you meeting him?" Dave asked, picking up my stapler and twirling it around.

"At Machiavelli's up by St. Paul's," I replied, taking the stapler from his hands and replacing it on the desk, only to have him pick up my hole punch instead. "I will know which kleptomaniac to come after if I come in tomorrow and there are stationery items missing," I warned him with a grin.

Dave simply laughed, putting the hole punch back in its place, and swiped my favorite pen instead. I shook my head at him. He was incorrigible.

"We'll be at The Tower if you wanna meet after," Jimmy said, naming the pub closest to the office as we walked towards the bank of lifts to take us down to the lobby entrance of the building.

"Okay, see you there in fifteen minutes," I said, only half joking. Seriously, I was going to get this over and done with as quickly as possible.

***

The rain had stopped and the early evening sun bathed the city in a soft glow. The old fashioned wrought iron streetlamps that lined the road towards St. Paul's Cathedral hadn't yet turned on. Machiavelli's was on a corner and had floor-to-ceiling plate glass windows wrapping around both street views. It was already busy for a Wednesday night, with groups of men and women dressed in business attire gathered around tables chatting and laughing.

I stepped off the street and entered through the open doors. The bar itself was brightly lit with strings of tiny lights draped from one corner of the room to the other and back again forming a crisscross pattern across the entire ceiling. The heels of my shoes beat out a loud rap on the polished wooden floor, as I walked towards the bar, my eyes scanning the room. Andrew had said that William Johnston was tall and dark-haired. "You should have made him wear a rose," I had suggested to Andrew as I was leaving the office, which had only earned me a glare; at this rate summer would be turning into autumn.

Ah, that had to be him, leaning against the bar, fiddling with his mobile phone. He was tall, as Andrew had described, with thick dark hair, which curled over his collar and hung across his forehead. He was well dressed in a dark blue suit. As if aware of my scrutiny, he straightened up and looked towards me with a questioning tilt of his head. Over-confident, I thought, deciding in that instant that I disliked him. I stopped in front of him.

"William?" I asked, returning his cool questioning gaze.

"You must be Jessica." His accent was English, well-educated. I shook his hand. "Call me Will. Can I get you a drink?"

"I think it's me that's supposed to offer that. What can I get you?" I asked.

"A Becks then, please, Jessica," he replied leaning back against the bar and studying me.

I signaled to the nearest barman. "A bottle of Becks and a skinny gin and tonic please."

We found a couple of empty armchairs in one corner and Will turned on the charm. First, he helped me take my raincoat off and laid it over the back of my chair, then he waited until I had sat down before taking a seat himself. Old manners, unusual in the politically correct equal opportunity business world, but still, I refused to be charmed. I wasn't here to make friends. Will adjusted the cuffs of his pale blue double-cuff shirt beneath his suit jacket. His cufflinks were gold dice; I noted the satirical choice for a career in investment banking, where so much was speculative.

"So, what's this then? Get me drunk and see if I will spill all my deep, dark secrets?" He smiled.

"Actually, it would save me a lot of time and money, if we can skip the drunken bit and you just tell me your secrets," I replied.

Will leaned forward and looked up at me with a glint in his blue eyes. "So, Jessica, what exactly *would* you like to know?"

I spluttered on my drink. Holy crap, this guy was super confident. Flirting with the interviewer didn't usually get you a job.

I sat back in my chair and tried to adopt a neutral expression and ignore the fact that he had my attention. "Well, why don't you tell me a bit about yourself?"

"Okay, I grew up in Sussex. Obtained my Maths degree from UCL and Chartered Accountancy with EY," he answered. "But I'm sure you know all that."

I had expected him to wax lyrical about himself, given that I had left him with such an open-ended question. The fact that he didn't, showed he was clever. There was more to him than just the charm. I finished my drink as we chatted a little about the work he had done and who we both knew at EY.

"Anyway, enough about me. How did a nice Scottish girl like you end up working in the cut-throat world of investment banking?" Will asked.

Okay, so maybe I was wrong. There was that awful charm again.

"Who said anything about me being nice?" I growled.

Will, to his credit, laughed and raised his empty bottle. "Next round is definitely on me," he said.

I looked at my watch and acquiesced. It would be rude to end the interview after just twenty minutes, even if I did consider it a farce. "Okay, but just one. I have to get going."

Will nodded and made his way to the bar. I watched him go. He had broad shoulders and carried himself in a way that spoke of someone at ease in their own skin. He stopped and shook hands with a guy standing at a tall table and leaned over, kissing the cheek of the woman with him. As much as I hated to admit it, he would be a good fit in the team. Easy to get on with and charming enough to deal with the odd difficult trader. I didn't have to like him. Hell, I didn't really have to even work with him. My job here was done.

"So. What else are you supposed to glean from me tonight?" he asked with a grin as he placed my drink on the little table between our chairs.

I sat twisting my wedding and engagement rings around on my finger. "Nothing, I think I'm done. I guess you'll be hearing from Andrew tomorrow. Do you have any questions for me?"

Will tilted his head, a little smile playing around his lips. "Just one."

"Sure, fire away."

"Will you have dinner with me?" he asked.

I wasn't expecting that. "No," I replied, trying not to sound prim. "You do realize that I am married?"

Will nodded and shrugged his shoulders. "Just thought I'd ask," he replied.

* * *

I arrived at The Tower around eight pm. The doors of the old pub were wide open and Jimmy and Dave were holding court out front, surrounded by a group of people. From the peals of laughter coming from their audience, it sounded like they were trying to outdo each other with the funniest anecdotes; nothing new there. Jimmy caught my eye as I walked closer and broke away from the group to greet me.

"Hey, Jess, how did it go? William? Verdict?" he asked.

"He has the charm of a prince and the morals of an alley cat. He will be a perfect fit," I answered.

Jimmy looked stunned for a moment, before a grin spread across his face. "Did he try to hit on you?"

I must have looked uncomfortable because he slipped a friendly arm around my shoulders and turned me towards the doors leading into the bar.

"Didn't you tell him about the strapping Scotsman that you have tucked away at home?"

I laughed. "No, it wasn't like that."

Jimmy signaled to the barman. "My friend here needs a G and T pronto."

The barman obliged, upending a blue bottle into a measuring cup just as a loud boom sounded and the pub shook. The cup slipped from the barman's fingers with a clatter. Bottles in the refrigerators behind the counter and those on the shelf against the wall behind the bar rattled. Empty glasses tipped over on an adjacent table and several bottles of spirits skidded off the end of the bar, splintering into shards as they hit the wooden floor. Clear liquid ran across the boards following the slope of the floor towards the door.

With a shriek, I grabbed on to the edge of the bar for support.

There was an eerie silence for a moment as everyone looked at each other with a mixture of confusion and concern.

"What the hell was that?" Jimmy said. "An earthquake?"

"Jim," Dave shouted from outside.

Jimmy and I looked at each other for a second before rushing through the door to join Dave.

"Look." He pointed up the road to where an enormous cloud of smoke and dust rose into the dusky sky. The screech of brakes sounded as traffic pulled to an abrupt stop on the busy road. Then loud splintering crashes could be heard as brick, timber and metal returned to earth and the awful sound of human suffering rose above the din.

We started running up the road in the direction of the blast. Jimmy and Dave, not hampered by shoes with three inch heels, raced ahead of me, covering the two blocks in no time. By the time I joined them, the first survivors were staggering from what remained of the Kings Arms Hotel, covered in white powder from fractured concrete and plaster.

"What the—" began Dave.

We stood frozen to the spot and watched as two figures stepped from the rubble into the road, leaning on one another to stay upright. Both had blood running down their faces from cuts to their heads. Behind them a woman took a few lurching steps before collapsing beside a broken wooden bar stool with a feeble cry for help. A dazed man stepped over her, crossed the road and kept walking, his gaze unfocused. Two young women stumbled out of the wreckage, clinging to one another, their clothes torn and dusty, each missing a high-heeled shoe, so that they appeared to be engaged in an elaborate twisting dance routine. A man pushed past them calling for help, blood squirting from beneath the hand he pressed into his shoulder where his arm would once have been. Another man remained seated at an outdoor table, his hand still wrapped around a half-full pint of beer. On his lap sat one of the pub's many colorful hanging baskets, the reds, blues and greens of the flowers and foliage in stark contrast to the chalky white powder which covered the man's hair and clothes. What remained of his drinking companions lay scattered around him, like a macabre human jigsaw. The man stared into space with a blank expression.

"Oh my God," I said, covering my mouth with my hand as I took in the horrific scene, struggling to comprehend the wreckage.

All around us people began rising from where they had taken cover moments earlier. There were desperate shouts as some hurried towards the wounded, whilst others held back, unsure what to do faced with such devastation. As I looked around, I noticed some people begin filming the carnage on their mobile phones.

Dave rushed forward and took the arm of one of the young women, while Jimmy went to the aid of her friend and helped them to sit down on the edge of the curb. They were shaking uncontrollably, so I took my raincoat off and draped it around the shoulders of the one nearest to me.

The wail of sirens from emergency responders racing to the scene began to get louder as they approached from all directions. A single police car pulled to a stop beside us and two young police officers alighted, donning their hats as they stepped out. Their faces displayed horrified expressions as they surveyed the chaos, but these were soon replaced by grim determination as they strode forward and took charge. One officer directed those of us helping the injured to lead them to an open outdoor square across the road from the scene, whilst the second officer tried to contain the spectators.

"Help is on the way," he called. "We need to make certain that there isn't a second device or a gas leak before going in." Jimmy, who'd been climbing into the rubble to assist the injured, now stepped back and looked around with a helpless expression. "I know," the officer said understanding his reaction. "But until we know what we are dealing with we don't want any further casualties."

"It was a car bomb," a man in the growing crowd called out, pointing to the almost unrecognizable mangled remains of a vehicle lying on its side up against the broken windows of a neighboring building, which until a few minutes earlier had been a lunch-time sandwich bar. "I saw it light up seconds before the explosion."

"Okay, sir. Don't go anywhere. We'll need a statement from you," the officer replied before relaying the information through to headquarters on his shoulder-mounted radio.

"Jessica." I turned towards the voice. Will jogged across the road to join me. "Are you okay?"

"These poor people, they were just having a drink like we were earlier," I said, wringing my hands and watching as a team of fireman leapt from their truck, unwinding a hose to deal with a small blaze that smoldered at the rear of the site.

Will nodded. "I know."

I looked up at him. His brow was furrowed and he looked as distraught as I felt.

"Who would do such a thing? In the heart of London?" I asked.

Jimmy and Dave returned from helping the two young women to an ambulance that had just arrived. Dave handed me back my raincoat.

"Will, this is Jimmy and Dave, two of your new colleagues," I said.

"G'day, mate," Jimmy said as he hurried past us and back towards the remains of the pub. "Can you give us a hand with this guy?" he called over his shoulder.

"Sure," Will replied, following him and taking the other side of a solidly built injured man who had staggered from the pub. Between them, Jimmy and Will helped him across the road to the square where more ambulances and paramedics were beginning to arrive.

The smell of smoke and rotten wood intermingled with something sweet and sickly hit me as I helped an older woman away from the debris to relative safety. I wrinkled my nose and looked skywards; sunset was upon us. I noticed a police van arrive and several officers begin setting up spotlights on tripods pointed at what remained of the pub.

We were busy for the next twenty minutes, helping the walking wounded from the ruins across the road to the square to be triaged and assisting the small handful of police officers to set up barriers until more of their colleagues arrived. At one point I found myself moving odd shoes, bags, documents and other personal objects thrown by the blast into the street, to an area at the edge of the square. The bomb squad arrived and we were all moved back from the site. We were beginning to feel surplus to requirements when a police officer approached us.

"Anyone else is going to need either a stretcher or a body bag," he said with a grim expression. "Thanks for your assistance, but I'll need you back behind the barrier now. Leave your details with the officer over there as we'll need statements from you all."

We nodded and walked across to the officer holding a tablet, at the edge of police cordon, and gave our names and contact details. I looked down at my white shirt; it had a blood stain on the sleeve and black marks across the front. I went to pull my raincoat on but noticed that it had drops of blood across the shoulders. I shuddered. I looked at my hands, they were blackened too. I hiccupped, the beginnings of a sob.

"Come on," Jimmy said, taking my arm. "Let's head back to The Tower, I need a stiff drink after that. Will, mate, join us?"

* * *

As we ducked under the hastily erected police cordon, a block back from the scene we noticed Aditi Sharma, the petite dark-haired BBC reporter, standing alongside the crews of several other television networks, awaiting the signal from her cameraman as he counted her in. We paused to listen.

"I'm reporting live from the scene of a devastating terrorist attack in the heart of London tonight." Aditi paused and looked behind her at the remains of the pub, a smoldering pile of brick and plaster, dotted with a number of white sheets, covering the bodies of the dead. "Eye witnesses tell me that a car bomb exploded outside the Kings Arms Hotel on Cheapside at 8.05 pm tonight. No one has yet claimed responsibility for the attack at one of the City's popular after work venues. There is currently no official death toll, but I understand that there are already eighteen confirmed dead and many more injured."

Aditi pressed her right hand to the earpiece in her ear as the news anchor in the studio asked her a question. A moment later she nodded.

"Another incidence of home grown terror? We're hearing those rumors here too. This is the third attack since the outcome of the Brexit referendum, but as yet there's been no official comment. Witnesses describe the two men who parked the van containing the bomb and walked away ten minutes before the explosion, as white and in their twenties. We understand that police teams are pulling the street CCTV footage as we speak."

She paused, listening before continuing. "At this point no one has claimed responsibility, so we have no idea as to the motive behind the attack, but there is some speculation that this incident may be related to the recent Trafalgar Square and Windsor bombings. However, it does seem that this was a much larger device, so authorities will be desperately hoping that this isn't an escalation of violence."